SAINT ANTHONY
AND OTHER STORIES

SAINT ANTHONY
AND OTHER STORIES

by Guy de Maupassant

Selected and Translated
by Lafcadio Hearn

Edited with an Introduction
by Albert Mordell

Short Story Index Reprint Series

BOOKS FOR LIBRARIES PRESS
FREEPORT, NEW YORK

First Published 1924
Reprinted 1971

INTERNATIONAL STANDARD BOOK NUMBER:
0-8369-3820-8

LIBRARY OF CONGRESS CATALOG CARD NUMBER:
79-150479

PRINTED IN THE UNITED STATES OF AMERICA

CONTENTS

INTRODUCTION

Lafcadio Hearn was employed on the New Orleans *Times-Democrat* from December, 1881, to June, 1887. One of his chief duties was to make translations from the French for the Sunday edition. These translations, which Hearn did not sign except on one or two occasions, ranged from one to two columns of closely printed type and appeared under the heading, "The Foreign Press." Both his biographers, Mrs. Elizabeth Bisland Wetmore and Nina H. Kennard, in their biographies, assign all these translations to Hearn. The newspaper itself several times stated that Hearn was the translator. More than one-half of these translations are listed by title in the bibliography of Dr. George M. Gould's *Concerning Lafcadio Hearn*. This bibliography was made up from Hearn's own scrapbook. This scrapbook was unfortunately lost and as the bibliography contains no dates of the original translations from the *Times-Democrat*, I had to spend many hours in the Congressional Library over the yellow pages of the bound volumes of that newspaper to get the dates of the Maupassant stories in order to have them photostated. I found about fifty of them, although Gould mentions only about thirty.

It should be remembered that these are the first,* besides

* Hearn anticipated the first collection of Maupassant in book form, *The Odd Number* (1889).

being the best and most artistic translations of Maupassant. Hearn who incidentally was of the same age as Maupassant, translated the tales as soon as they appeared in periodical or book form. He intended issuing, after the publication of his translation from Gautier, several volumes of translations from French authors, including one from Maupassant. His idea was to embody a style of a school, as he wrote to a friend. Gould also intended issuing a volume of miscellaneous translations, but such a venture was impossible after the controversy following the publication of his book. The loss of the scrapbook also seemed a hindrance to such a future project. This loss has, however, not been irremediable. I have been fortunate in locating all the Maupassant translations done by Hearn.

The publication of this volume, therefore, carries out what was originally Hearn's own plan. Lack of encouragement and leisure prevented this plan from being feasible in his own life.

Hearn also published four editorials on Maupassant, or his work, and collected these in book form for the first time last year in *Essays on European and Oriental Literature*. The editorial on the story, *Solitúde*, is exceptionally fine. "The faithfulness of his translations from the French," says one of his biographers, "and the beauty of the style of some of his contributions, had found an appreciative circle in the Crescent City, and a clique had been formed of what were known as 'Hearn's admirers.'" (Nina Kennard.)

No other French author appealed to Hearn as much as

Maupassant, with the possible exception of Loti. Hearn always retained his admiration for Maupassant and frequently mentioned him in his lectures to his Japanese students, and in his letters to B. H. Chamberlain. "Maupassant is the greatest realist who ever lived, greater even than Merimée" (*Life and Literature*, page 263); "the greatest story teller that the European world has ever known" (page 265). He dwells on Maupassant's impersonal suggestive method, on his ability to convey an emotion without the use of words descriptive of the emotion, on his impressionistic manner in relating a story without any beginning or end, and regards "his commentaries and arguments as the most valuable part of his work" (*Japanese Letters*, page 367). Nevertheless Hearn recognized that Maupassant was at times disgusting and did not possess deep human sympathy, nor did he sympathize with the Frenchman's pessimistic outlook.

A final word as to these translations. They are first faithful and artistic. They are in a certain sense creative themselves. They are done in masterly English and their superiority may be seen by a comparison with the usual translations found in some of the collected editions of Maupassant in English. Rarely has such noble work been done in a newspaper. This volume also represents the better work of Maupassant. Although Hearn's personal later opinion was that Maupassant never excelled his first story, *Boule-de-Suif* (Ball of Fat), there can be no question that here we have great stories that were written by a creative artist and translated by a man who was a poet.

One cannot understand Hearn, the creative artist, unless one makes a study of his theories and work as a translator. The tales he told over from stories orally related to him in Japan were really bits of creative and artistic translation. They were lineally descended from his first work as a translator, when in the early hours of the morning, after his newspaper work in Cincinnati was done, he pegged away on his translations of Gautier. The admirers of Hearn need not be amazed that this genius should have given so much time and energy to translation when he could have done original work. For the step from artistic translation to retelling tales of which the plot had been furnished to him by reading or orally, was hardly a perceptible one. Moreover, he did not have to infuse much of his personality into the stories he translated, because he chose only such stories wherein his personality had already found a mirror. Nor need we pay any attention to those carping critics who wish to underestimate Hearn by maintaining that he had no originality and would be remembered only as a translator. Hearn used plots and recreated them just as Shakespeare did. The style, ideas and the whole tenor of his adapted tales as in *Chinese Ghosts* make the stories beautiful, original works of art; they adorn and improve the original sources. When *Stray Leaves from Strange Literature* appeared in 1884 the critics were puzzled as to whether the stories were original or translations. They are both, might be the answer. Hearn himself admitted in his preface to that book that some of the tales were literal translations from the French prose version of the *Kalevala*. Other tales were so freely reconstructed that they were his own in every sense of the word.

So in his first book, the translation from *One of Cleopatra's Nights* (1882), we have already the Hearn we know. It took him four years to find a publisher and he defrayed part of the expenses of publication of that volume. Why was Hearn so eager for its appearance if he had not felt that the translated book was as much part of himself as it was of Gautier? In a sense, Hearn, the writer of tales, remained a translator all his life, but he was never the mere transcriber. In fact someone who gave him the material for one of his later Japanese tales complained that Hearn introduced his own version in such a manner that it differed from the tale as originally told him. Hearn, the creative artist and teller of tales, was then not much different from Hearn, the translator. And yet as a translator he took no appreciable liberties with his text, but merely chose the best and most artistic English idiom into which to translate the French or Spanish he was translating.

The only other translation by Hearn that was issued in his lifetime in book form was that made of Anatole France's *Crime of Sylvestre Bonnard* (1890), done in a few weeks for a small sum for Harper's. He did this in New York before he went to Japan, and as usual was later not proud of his book. Yet his version remains the standard one, and appears in the complete English translation of Anatole France's works. His translation from Flaubert's *Temptation of St. Anthony,* made also in his Cincinnati days, in the middle seventies, could not find a publisher and appeared posthumously after the manuscript was recovered about a dozen years ago.

Hearn was really a crank on the subject of good translation. Time and time again in *The Item* * and in the *Times-Democrat* he attacked the spurious inartistic, inaccurate and incomplete translations made from the French novels in his day, especially of Zola. Publishers and translators wrote remonstrating letters to the *Times-Democrat.* Hearn replied to these editorially and once said that a publisher who gave out such products was cheating the public as much as any merchant who sold adulterated, for genuine, merchandise. He also recognized that only creative writers could make good translations and such authors preferred to do wholly original work; hence good translations were rare. In an editorial on the subject, reprinted by Dr. Gould, he showed what keen literary and prophetic insight he had as to the men best qualified to make translations, when he suggested what a fortunate thing it would be if a man like Henry James translated Alphonse Daudet. And only a few years later James, who certainly did not get the New Orleans *Times-Democrat* in England and who therefore never read of the suggestion, translated Daudet's *Port Tarascon.*

* Three of these editorials in *The Item* are: *Translations and Mutilations,* January 30, 1880; *Some American Translations,* January 30, 1881, and *How Stirling Translates Zola,* January 31, 1881.

Hearn believed in the fidelity of translations and was very much against verse translations of poems; he approved the French method of translating verse from a foreign language into prose. He pleaded for the translation of the Ancient Classics into good English prose, and approved of the *Lang et al.* translations of Homer. He was especially bitter against the translation wherein the translator changed the language, meaning and ideas in order to get a needed rhyme or measure. It is unfortunate that he did not live to see some of the excellent prose translations in the Loeb Classical Library from the Ancient Classical poets. And I doubt if he would have approved even of Gilbert Murray's verse translations. Hearn himself made a few attempts of prose translations from French verse. One from Baudelaire is published in Elisabeth Bisland's *Life and Letters.*

The excellent quality of Hearn's translations is attested by the fact that they were widely copied. On several occasions also the *Times-Democrat* registered complaints that the exchange papers, who copied the translations, did not give due credit to it by acknowledging the source. Hearn himself apparently wrote these complaints, in which he also said that the translations "entail considerable expense and trouble in the securing of good material."

All the translations in this volume except the second, *Simon's Papa*, appeared in the *Times-Democrat* from 1883 to 1887. My accidental discovery of this story is worth detailing, because of the simultaneous discovery of a large collection of translations and book reviews by Hearn not known hitherto to Hearn students. Gould mentions *Simon's Papa* among the Maupassant translations from the *Times-Democrat* he had in Hearn's scrapbook. I could not, however, find the story in the *Times-Democrat*. As the original story appeared in Maupassant's *Le Maison Tellier*, published in 1881, I thought the story possibly was translated for *The Item*, for Hearn was employed on that paper the first eleven months of 1881. When I looked through the files of *The Item* in New Orleans last winter, I found that Hearn had done only about a dozen translations for that paper in the three and a half years he was connected with it, and there was no translation there from Maupassant. There was a translation in *The Item* from Daudet, and another from Zola, and both of these are mentioned in Gould's book as being from the *Times-Democrat*. I also found two of Gautier's stories, which were later collected in *One of Cleopatra's Nights* (*Mummy's Foot*, June 16 and 23, 1878, and *Arria Marcella*, September 6 to 11, inclusive, 1878), thus discovering for the first time where some of these Gautier translations originally appeared.

I gave up all hope of finding the Maupassant story for which I was looking. I felt sure, however, Hearn must have translated it for some New Orleans paper in 1881. I recalled his having written once to Krehbiel that one of the Gautier stories *Candaules* later published in *One of Cleopatra's Nights* was running serially in 1880 in some New Orleans paper, whose name he does not mention. In another letter of about the same period he wrote he might do translations for some literary paper to be founded at the same time while he was working for *The Item*. I also had been puzzled by the fact that while looking through the translations in the *Times-Democrat* I did not come arcoss many that were mentioned in Gould's list. The only alternative remained that Hearn had been doing translations for some paper in New Orleans in 1880 and 1881. But what paper? There were several papers in the city at that time. There was *The Times*, there was *The Democrat*, before they became consolidated in December, 1881. I picked up at random in the Cabildo, in New Orleans, a volume of *The Democrat* for 1881 and found there were translations in the Sunday issues under the title "Foreign Press"; all the translations having Hearn's characteristic punctuation, especially semicolons followed by dashes. I discovered many that were mentioned in Gould's list. I felt that here I would find the missing Maupassant story. And that is just what happened. I found the story in the issue for September 18, 1881.

I also saw that Hearn had begun contributing weekly translations to *The Democrat* May 23, 1880, till that paper was consolidated with *The Times*. All this time he was on *The Item* for which he was writing editorials almost daily. We see now how his connection as a translator for *The Democrat* for a year and a half led to his employment on the *Times-Democrat*. Two Hearn myths are also thus disposed of, namely, that Hearn was an idler, and that he went to the

Times-Democrat without previous connection with either of the two papers from which it was consolidated. In fact, Hearn only continued on the *Times-Democrat* a department, "The Foreign Press," which he had conducted for a year and a half on *The Democrat*.

In that year and a half Hearn was studying Spanish and he did much translation from that language for *The Democrat*. What is also not known is that his first translations from Loti, and from Anatole France's, *The Crime of Sylvestre Bonnard*, and Flaubert's, *The Temptation of St. Anthony*, originally appeared in *The Democrat*.

In a book review by Hearn in *The Democrat* (May 8, 1881), I found some of Hearn's own views on the subject of translation. He wrote:

"To translate well it is more important that the translator be a perfect master of the tongue *into* which the translation is made than of that *from* which it is to be made. In brief, the artistic translator must have control over his own idiom: he must be able to reproduce the most delicate shade of feeling and expression in the original; he must be able to transplant the rarest flowers of the exotic language into the best soil of his own, and skilfully acclimate them so that nothing of their performance and strange charm will be lost."

In a book review of Hearn's Gautier volume, published in the *Times-Democrat*, March 26, 1882, and written by some personal friend who incorporated Hearn's views on translation (received no doubt by word of mouth) we have the following passage:

"In every work of art that is worth anything, whether in painting or literature, there must be life and soul. The great difficulty in copying and translating is to seize the living idea, that essence which has no tangible form, which is seen and yet eludes the grasp, which resplends through the painting or the poem, strikingly tantalizing and yet so desperately perplexing to the copyist or translator."

It would possibly be no exaggeration to say that no one has ever translated from the French into the English so well as Hearn. Edward Thomas, in his monograph on Hearn says, speaking of Hearn's translation from Gautier: "A better translation is not likely to be made, because a man capable of doing it better would probably leave it alone and do original work." And there have been French students who regarded Hearn's translations as better than the original.

In the six and a half years Hearn was on the *Times-Democrat* he made about three hundred translations. About one-sixth of these were from Maupassant, so that he translated more from Maupassant than he did from any other author.

After he left the paper in the first week in June, 1887, French translations continued to appear in the paper but evidently not from his pen. I found five translations from Maupassant, but without Hearn's characteristic punctuation, that is, semicolons or dashes. These stories are as follows: *A Christmas Story*, June 5, 1887; *The Devil*, July 10; *Love*,

July 24; *The Inn*, August 14; and *A Widow*, October 3. I have not included these as Mrs. Julie K. W. Baker, widow of the Sunday Editor, Mr. Marion Baker, informs me that after Hearn left the paper, his regular department ceased as it was realized no one could replace him, and that no translations, after he left, are his.

Mrs. Baker herself continued doing the literary editorials, beginning with one on Stevenson, June 5, 1887. She also translated from the French.

It is possible that one of these five stories from Maupassant (*A Christmas Story*) may be Hearn's. Words and phrases like "festoons," "ghost-like" fields, "wan" moon, "pallid desolation," are certainly Hearnian.

However, as some doubt is raised as to the Hearn authorship by Mrs. Baker's letter, I have omitted this story along with the other four, so that the reader can feel absolutely sure that every story in this volume was translated by Hearn.

The appearance of this volume is in no way intended to conflict with the recent publication, both in America and England, of new complete translations of Maupassant. The value of this work is in the fact that it is a Hearn product, that it is a genius translator's version of a genius short-story writer.

ALBERT MORDELL.

Philadelphia,
April 14, 1924.

SAINT ANTHONY

SAINT ANTHONY
AND OTHER STORIES

SAINT ANTHONY

THEY called him Saint Anthony, partly because his name was Anthony, partly because he was a jovial, joyous old fellow, who liked his joke—a good trencher man and a deep drinker, although he was over sixty. He was a fine, tall countryman, stout and broad-shouldered and high coloured, with long legs that seemed too lanky for such a heavy body.

He was a widower, and lived alone on his farm with his two farm labourers and a servant girl. He managed the farm himself like a smart master as he was, careful of his own interests, a good hand at business, and well up in the breeding of beasts and the cultivation of his land. His two sons and three daughters, who were all well married and lived in the neighbourhood, always came to dine with him once a month. His colossal strength was celebrated in all the country round, so that "He is as strong as Saint Anthony" had become proverbial!

At the time of the Prussian invasion, Saint Anthony would boast, as he sat drinking in the public house, that he would eat up one of their armies if they came his way, for he was a true Normand for boasting, something of a coward withal,

3

and blustering. He would thump his fists on the wooden table till he made the cups and glasses dance; again, he would sit there, with his red face and cunning eyes, and, making a show of anger, declare: "I could eat 'em without salt!" He had reckoned the Prussians would never get as far as Tanneville; but when he heard they were at Rantôt he shut himself up in his house and never went out, and all day long he watched the road from the little window in his kitchen, expecting every moment to see the bayonets go past.

One morning, as he was at breakfast with all his household, the door opened and in walked maître Chicot, the mayor, followed by a soldier with a black helmet, with a brass point on his head. Saint Anthony sprang up out of his chair. The farm people watched him, expecting him to fall upon the Prussian, but he only shook hands with the mayor, as he said to him:

"Here's one for you, Saint Anthony. They come last night. And don't 'ee play no fules' tricks, for they talk of shootin' and burnin' everything for the least thing as goes wrong. So now ye're warned. Gie 'un summat to eat, he looks a good 'un enough. Good day. I'm goin' 'round to the others. There's one for each on em." And he went out.

Father Anthony, very pale, looked at his Prussian. The soldier was a stout, young fellow, fat and fair, with blue eyes and a light brown beard that covered the whole of his cheeks. He looked foolish and shy and good-natured. The sly Normand read him at a glance, and, much relieved, signed to him to sit down. "Will you have some soup?" The stranger did not understand. Then Anthony tried a bold stroke; he pushed a plateful of soup under his nose, and cried: "There, swallow that down, great pig."

The soldier answered, "Ya," and began to eat greedily, while the triumphant farmer, feeling that he had saved his reputation, winked at his servants, who made strange grimaces, trying to smother their laughter.

When the Prussian had emptied his plateful, Saint Anthony filled it again, and he emptied it a second time, but at the third helping he refused. The farmer tried to force him to eat it, repeating: "Come now, eat it up: we'll fatten you or we'll know the reason why, my pig!"

And the soldier, who only understood that they wanted him to eat as much as he could, laughed pleasantly, and made signs that he had enough.

Then Saint Anthony, who began to grow quite familiar, poked him in the ribs, crying: "My piggy has had a good breakfast!" But all of a sudden he turned purple, and began to choke, unable to speak, convulsed with laughter at a thought that had just struck him: "I have it, I have it; Saint Anthony and his pig. There's my pig." And the three servants burst into a roar of laughter.

The old man was so delighted that he called for some of his best brandy and offered it all round to everybody. They all hob-nobbed with the Prussian, who smacked his lips out of politeness to show that he thought it excellent. And Saint

Anthony shouted in his ear: "Hein, there's something worth drinking. You don't get that at home, my piggy."

From that time Father Anthony never stirred out without his Prussian. That was his revenge, sly old rogue that he was. And the whole countryside, in spite of their fears, roared with laughter at Saint Anthony's joke. When the invaders had their backs turned he was a rare hand at a joke; not another man in the country could have invented a trick like that.

And every afternoon he used to go round to the neighbours arm in arm with his German, and introduce him, slapping him gaily on the back and crying: "Here he is, my pig, he fattens up finely, don't he?"

And the peasants would grin all around. "Bless his merry old soul, old Anthony," said they.

"I'll sell him to thee, Césaire, for three pistoles."

"I'll take him, Anthony, and invite you to come and taste the black-puddings."

"What I'd like would be his feet."

"Just feel his ribs, you see he is nothing but fat."

And they winked at each other, and laughed, but not too loud, for fear the Prussian should begin to see that they made a laughing-stock of him. Only Anthony, who grew bolder and bolder every day, would poke him in the ribs and cry, "Nothing but fat," and lift him in his arms with the strength of a giant, shouting: "He weighs six hundred, and not an ounce of waste."

He made a habit of having his pig fed wherever he went. Every day that was the great joke, the grand entertainment: "Give him whatever you like; it is all fish that comes to his net." And they offered the man bread and butter, potatoes, cold pudding, or, better still, chitterlings, that gave them the opportunity of recommending them as "Your own, and of the best."

The soldier, who was stupid and gentle, pleased at the attentions they showed him, ate everything out of politeness, and made himself ill rather than refuse; and he really did get fatter so that he could hardly fasten his uniform, to the great delight of Saint Anthony, who kept repeating: "You will have to get another cage made for you, Piggy."

At the same time they were really fast friends; and when the old man had business in the neighbourhood, the Prussian went with him of his own accord, for the pleasure he had in his society.

The weather was very severe; it froze hard; the terrible winter of 1870 added another scourge to those that already chastened the country.

Father Anthony, who was far-sighted and knew how to take advantage of his opportunities, foreseeing that there would be a scarcity of manure that spring, bought a lot of manure of a neighbour who happened to be in difficulties, and arranged with him that he was to bring his cart every evening and fetch away a cartload.

So every evening he used to set off to the Haules farm,

about a mile and a half away, always accompanied by his pig. And every day there was the grand entertainment of seeing the animal fed. The whole neighbourhood used to turn out to see it as regularly as they went to high mass on a Sunday.

The soldier, however, began to get suspicious, and when they laughed too long and too loudly he rolled his eyes restlessly, and they flashed with anger from time to time.

Now, one evening when he had eaten as much as he cared for, he refused to swallow another morsel, and he got up to leave the place. But Saint Anthony seized him by the wrist and, putting his two powerful hands on his shoulders, pushed him down into his chair so heavily that the chair crashed to the ground under him.

There was a perfect storm of merriment. Old Anthony was radiant. He picked up his pig, pretended to rub him down to make him well, and then swore: "Since thee wilt not eat, thee shall drink!" And they sent out to the public-house for some brandy.

The soldier looked around the room angrily, but he drank all the same; he drank as much as they would, and Saint Anthony kept him in countenance, to the great joy of the company.

The Normand, as red as a tomato, and with his eyes inflamed, filled the glasses, and hob-nobbed, shouting "Your health!" And the Prussian, without a word, gulped down great tumblers of brandy.

It was a struggle, a battle, a match! They drank one against the other. They were both of them about at the end of their tether by the time the bottle was finished; but neither of them was beaten. It was a drawn game, that was all; they would begin again to-morrow.

They staggered out, and began to walk home, by the side of the cart of manure that was dragged slowly along by two horses.

There was no moon, but the snow, which had begun to fall, lighted the night with the glare of its dead whiteness. The cold penetrated the two men and increased their drunkenness; Saint Anthony, who was cross at not having won his match, amused himself by pushing his pig from time to time by the shoulder, and trying to make him fall into the ditch. Each time the other drew back to avoid his attack, muttering a few words in German in an angry tone, that only made the peasant burst out laughing. At last the Prussian really lost his temper, and the next time Anthony knocked up against him, he answered by a tremendous blow of his fist that almost knocked the giant down.

Then the old man, inflamed with brandy, seized the soldier in his arms, shook him as if he had been a child, and threw him with all his force to the other side of the road. Then, satisfied with this punishment, he crossed and stood laughing.

But the soldier got up directly, bare headed, for his helmet had fallen off, and, drawing his sword rushed upon old Anthony. When he saw him approach the peasant seized his whip, a great cart whip of holly wood, straight, and strong, and supple and held it by the middle ready to strike.

The Prussian ran at him with his head down and his sword drawn to kill him. But the old man seized the naked blade in his hand and turning aside the point, struck his adversary a tremendous blow on the forehead with the handle of his whip that felled him to the ground.

Then, horror-stricken at what he had done, he stood staring stupidly at the body at his feet, that after a few convulsive spasms, lay motionless, face downward. He stooped down and turned the body over and looked at it; the man's eyes were shut, and a slender stream of blood trickled from a wound in his forehead. In spite of the darkness, old Anthony could make out the dark stain of the blood upon the snow.

He stood there, bewildered, while the horses went quietly on with the cart, in front of him.

What was to be done? He would be shot! His farm would be burnt down and the whole country ravaged! What should he do? What should he do? How was he to hide the body, to conceal the dead, and hoodwink the Prussians? He heard voices in the distance, in the silence of the snow. In desperation he picked up the helmet and replaced it on the head of his victim, then seized him in his arms, lifted him up and ran after the cart. When he overtook it he threw the body on to the top of the manure. As soon as he got home he would see what was to be done.

He walked slowly, cudgelling his brains, but finding no way

out of his dilemma. He could only see and feel that he was a lost man. He turned into the farmyard. There was a light burning in one of the attic windows, the servant was not gone to bed yet; he hastily backed the cart to the very edge of the dung-pit. He had reflected that if he upset the load into the pit, the body, being on the top, would fall in first, to the bottom of the hole; and he tilted up the cart.

As he had expected, the man was buried under the heap of manure. Anthony flattened and levelled it with his pitch-fork, which he then stuck into the ground near. He called the farm labourer to take the horses to the stable, and then he went indoors to his own room.

He went to bed, still turning over in his mind what was to be done, but not a single idea occurred to him, and he only grew more and more terrified as he lay there on his bed. They would shoot him! His teeth chattered, and a cold perspiration broke out all over him; at last he got up, shaking with fear; he could stand it no longer.

He went down to the kitchen, took a bottle of brandy out of the cupboard and came upstairs again. He drank two great tumblers, one after the other, but though they made him drunker than ever, they did nothing to drown the agony of his soul. He had done a fine stroke—a confounded fool!

He walked up and down his room, setting his craft to work to invent some story, and from time to time he swallowed a mouthful of brandy to try and keep his heart up.

But he could think of nothing, nothing.

Toward midnight his watchdog, a sort of wolfish creature he called "Dévorant," began to raise the death howl. It froze the very marrow in old Anthony's bones. Every time the beast set up that long and dismal howl the old man's blood ran cold with fear.

He had fallen into a chair, perfectly worn out and dazed, listening anxiously for each howl from "Dévorant," shaken to his very soul by all the terrors mortal men can feel.

The clock downstairs struck five. The dog had never ceased his howling. The old peasant felt as if he should go out of his mind. He got up to go and unchain the dog, not to hear him any more. He went downstairs, unfastened the door, and went out into the night.

The snow was still falling. Everything was white. The farm buildings stood out like great black spots. The man went up to the kennel. The dog was pulling at his chain. He let him loose. "Dévorant" gave a spring, then stopped suddenly, in front of the dunghill, with his hair bristling, his legs stiffened, and showing his teeth.

Saint Anthony, shaking from head to foot, stammered: "What's the matter then, you vile cur?" and he went forward a few steps, trying to pierce with his eyes the dim shadows that filled the court.

Then he saw a form, a human form sitting on his dunghill.

He looked at it breathless, and paralyzed with horror. Till suddenly he perceived the handle of his pitchfork sticking upright in the ground, he tore it out of the earth, in such a transport of fear as drives the veriest coward to the rashest deeds, and rushed forward to see what the figure was.

It was he, the Prussian. The warmth of the manure bed had brought him back to life again and he had crawled out from under it. He had seated himself there mechanically, and there he stayed, all covered with dirt and blood, with the snow falling softly upon him, still stupid with drink, stunned with the blow and weak from his wound.

He caught sight of Anthony and, still too stunned to remember anything, made a movement to rise from his seat. But the old man, as soon as he saw who it was, foamed with rage like some wild beast.

He stuttered out: "Ah! pig! pig! You are not dead. You think you are going to denounce me after all, do you! Wait a moment!"

And he flew at the German with his pitchfork and drove the four iron prongs into his chest, up to the handle.

The soldier fell back with a long dying groan, the old peasant pulling his weapon out of the wound, stuck it again and again into the still palpitating body, driving the pitchfork into the stomach and throat and head until it was a mass of wounds from head to foot, with the blood bubbling out of every wound.

Then he stopped, out of breath with the violent exertion, panting, pacified by the murder accomplished.

The cocks were beginning to crow in the fowlhouse, it would soon be broad daylight; he set to work to bury the man.

He hollowed out a hole in the manure, then dug a grave in the ground underneath it, working violently and irregularly, his arms and legs all going at once.

When the pit was deep enough, he rolled the dead body into it with a pitchfork, threw the earth on the top of it, stamped it well down and put the manure back into its place. He smiled as he saw the snow falling thickly and covering every trace with its white veil.

Then he stuck the pitchfork upright in the dung-heap and went back into the house. The bottle of brandy was still standing half full on the table. He emptied it at a draught, threw himself on his bed and went fast asleep.

He woke up quite sobered, calm and clear-headed, able to realize what had happened, and what would be the consequences.

An hour later he was flying all over the country inquiring for his soldier. He went to the officers to know, he said, why they had taken the man away from his house.

As his intimacy with the soldier was well known, no one suspected him, and it was even he who led the search for the Prussian, declaring that he used to go out gallivanting every evening.

An old retired gendarme in a neighbouring village, who kept an inn and had a pretty daughter, was arrested, and shot.

SIMON'S PAPA

SIMON'S PAPA

Mid-day had just struck. The school door opened and all the urchins rushed through it, jostling each other in order to get out more quickly. But instead of separating as usual and running home to dinner, they all stopped and stood a little way off, collected in groups, and began to whisper.

It was because that very morning Simon, the son of La Blanchette, had come to school for the first time.

Everybody had heard La Blanchette spoken of at home, and although she was well received in public, mothers treated her among themselves with a sort of slightly scornful compassion, which the children espied without in the least knowing why.

As for Simon, they did not know him, because he had never gone out much; and did not run about with them in the streets of the village along the banks of the river. Consequently, they had very little liking for him; and it was with a peculiar mingling of joy and astonishment that they had caught up and were repeating to one another the saying of a lad of fourteen or fifteen, who seemed to know a great deal, from the cunning way in which he winked his eyes.

"You know Simon? . . . Well, he's got no papa."

The son of La Blanchette finally appeared at the threshold.

He was a little wan, very clean, and looked very timid—almost clumsy.

He was about to go home to his mother when his assembled school fellows, still whispering and all staring at him with those malignant and cruel eyes that children have who are meditating some bad action, came up to him in groups, gradually surrounded him, and finally cut off his retreat altogether. He stood there in the middle, surprised and embarrassed without the least idea of what they were going to do to him. But the big boy who had brought the news, puffed up with his previous success, asked him:

"What's your name, you?" He answered, "Simon."

"Simon what?" persisted the other.

The child, quite confused, repeated: "Simon."

Then the lad cried out, "One must be Simon something . . . that's no name . . . Simon!"

And the little one, on the point of bursting into tears answered for the third time:

"My name is Simon."

The urchins began to laugh. The big lad shouted triumphantly, "Now you can see for yourselves that he hasn't got any papa." A great silence followed. The children were stupefied at this extraordinary, impossible, monstrous thing;— a boy who had no papa;—they stared at him as at a phenomenon, a being outside of nature's laws, and they all felt swelling within themselves that previously inexplicable contempt shown by their mothers for La Blanchette.

As for Simon, he leaned against a tree in order to keep himself from falling; and stood as if overwhelmed by some irreparable disaster. He sought some way of explaining himself. But he could think of nothing to answer them with, of no means of giving the lie to this frightful declaration that he had no papa. Finally, all livid, he cried out at random,— "Yes, I have one."

"Where is he?" queried the big boy.

Simon remained silent; he did not know. The children all laughed intensely excited by the novelty of the situation, and these sons of the fields, by nature nearer to animals than city children, all felt the cruel impulse which impels barnyard fowls to peck one of their own number to death the moment it is wounded. All at once Simon observed a little neighbour, the son of a widow, whom he had always seen, just like himself, all alone with his mother.

"And neither have you," he said, "you have no papa."

"Yes, I have, though," said the other.

"Where is he?" returned Simon.

"He is dead," replied the child with superb pride, "he is in the cemetery, my papa."

A murmur of applause arose from all the crowd of little scamps, as if the fact of having a dead father in the cemetery had made their comrade big enough to crush the other child who had no father at all. And the little blackguards, most of whose fathers were wicked, drunk, dishonest and brutal to their wives, jostled each other and drew together more compactly as though they wished to stifle to death the young unfortunate who lived outside of the general rule.

One who was pushed up right against Simon put out his tongue at him in a bantering way, and yelled:

"No papa!—no papa!"

Simon seized him by the hair with both hands and kicked him with all his might on the shins, while his enemy hit him savagely on the cheek. There was a great scuffle. The two combatants were separated, and Simon found himself beaten, torn, bruised and rolled on the ground in the midst of the circle of urchins who applauded his defeat. As he got up, mechanically trying with his hand to clean his little blouse, all dirty with dust, some one shouted to him:

"Now go and tell your papa about it!"

Then he felt, as it were, a great crumbling down in his heart. They were stronger than he; they had beaten him; and he could not answer them, for he knew that it was only too true he had no papa. Yet full of pride he tried a little while to struggle against the tears that were strangling him. He felt a sense of suffocation, and then began to cry silently with great sobs which violently shook his whole body.

Then the ferocious joy of his enemies burst forth, and quite naturally, just as certain savages do during their terrible fits of gaiety, they took each other by the hand and danced in a ring around him, singing in chorus: "No papa! No papa!" But Simon suddenly stopped sobbing. Rage drove him mad. There were stones lying at his feet; he picked them up and with all his force flung them at his torturers. Two or three were struck and ran away crying, and so formidable did he look that a panic seized the rest. Cowardly, as a crowd always becomes before an exasperated man, they dispersed and took to their heels.

Left alone, the little fatherless boy began to run through the field; for a sudden recollection had inspired him with a great resolution. He would drown himself in the river.

He remembered, in fact, that only eight days before, a poor fellow that used to beg for a living had thrown himself into the water because he could obtain no more money. Simon was there when they had fished him out, and the poor fellow, who had always seemed to him as dismal and ugly and dirty, had then impressed him greatly by his tranquil face with its pale cheeks, long wet beard, and calm open eyes. People standing around him said, "He's dead"; and somebody added, "Well, he's happy enough now." And Simon wanted to drown himself because he had no father just as the poor wretch did because he had no money.

He came to the brook, and got down close to the water and watched it flowing by. A few sporting fish glimmered in their rapid play through the clear current. Sometimes one would make a little leap and snap at the flies hovering about the surface. He stopped crying in order to look at them, for their little ways interested him very much. But from time to time, just as in the intervals of a tempest, come great squalls of wind, making the trees crackle, and passing by to die beyond the horizon—so this thought came to him with a sharp pain at his heart, "I am going to drown myself because I have no papa."

It was very warm, very pleasant. The mellow sunlight warmed the grass. The water shone like a mirror. And Simon felt moments of beatitude—of that languor which comes after tears, and he felt a great desire to lie down in the warm grass and sleep.

A little green frog jumped almost from under his feet. He tried to catch it; it escaped him. He ran after it and missed it three different times. At last he caught it by the extremity of one hind leg, and he laughed to see the efforts of the creature to escape. It would gather itself all up, doubling its long legs, and then with a spring suddenly stiffen them straight out like two bars; while with the golden circles of its eye larger than ever it beat the air vainly with its forelegs, as with hands. It made him think of a toy he had seen made of narrow strips of wood nailed in zigzag upon one another, which by one simultaneous movement caused little soldiers glued upon them to appear as if drilling. Then he thought of his home and of his mother; and seized with a great sorrow, he began to cry again. He trembled in every limb; he knelt down and tried to say his prayers, as if before going to sleep. But he could not finish them, for a fit of sobs came so violently and so tumultuously as to overwhelm him completely. He could not think, could not see anything around him, could only give himself wholly up to weeping.

Suddenly a heavy hand was laid upon his shoulder and a deep voice asked: "What is giving you so much trouble, little man?"

Simon looked around; a tall workman with a black beard and very curly black hair was looking down at him good-naturedly. He answered with eyes and voice full of tears:

"They beat me because . . . because . . . I have no . . . no papa . . . no papa!"

"How?" asked the man with a smile. "Why, everybody has one!"

Painfully the child answered through the spasms of his grief, "I . . . I . . . have none!"

Then the mechanic became serious; he had recognized the son of La Blanchette, and although a newcomer to that part of the country he already possessed a vague knowledge of her history.

"Come, my boy," he said, "cheer up! Come with me to your mamma. We'll find a papa for you."

They went along, the man taking the child by the hand; and the former smiled again, for he was not sorry to have this chance of seeing La Blanchette, who had the reputation of being one of the handsomest girls in the country; and perhaps, he thought to himself——

They stopped before a little house, very white, very clean. "Here it is," said the child; and he called out, "Mamma!"

A woman appeared and the mechanic suddenly ceased to smile; for he understood at once that there could be no foolish pleasantry with that tall, pale girl who stood severely at the door, as though to defend against all men the threshold of the house where another had betrayed her. Timidly, with cap in hand, he stammered in.

"Here, madame, I have brought you your little boy who lost his way near the river!"

But Simon sprang to his mother's neck and again bursting into tears, said:

"No, mamma, I wanted to drown myself because the others beat me . . . beat me . . . because I have no papa."

A scalding blush covered the young woman's cheeks, and wounded to the very quick of her being she kissed her child with passionate violence, while her tears fell upon his face. The man, deeply affected, remained there, not exactly knowing how to get away. But Simon suddenly ran to him and asked:

"Will you be my papa?"

A great silence followed. La Blanchette, stricken dumb, tortured with shame, leaned against the wall, pressing her hands over her heart. Receiving no answer the child continued:

"If you won't, I'll go back and drown myself."

The tall workman tried to pass it off as a joke, and answered with a laugh:

"Why, yes, little man, of course, I will."

"Then tell me your name," said the child, "so that I can tell the others when they ask me."

"Philip," replied the man. Simon remained silent a moment

in order to let the name get well into his head; then quite consoled he held out his arms, saying:

"Well, then, Philip, you are my papa."

The workman lifted him from the ground, kissed him quickly on both cheeks and strode away with great strides.

Next day when the child came into school a wicked laugh greeted him; and when recreation hour came, and the big boy wanted to commence again, Simon flung these words at his head, as he would have done a stone: "He is called Philip, my papa."

Yells of joy broke out on all sides.

"Philip who? Philip what? What sort of a name's that, Philip?—Where did you pick him up, your Philip?"

Simon did not answer, but immovable in his faith, he glared defiance at them all, ready to let himself be martyrized rather than to fly from them. The schoolmaster delivered him and he returned to his mother.

During these months tall Philip passed often before the house of La Blanchette, and sometimes when he saw her sewing at her window he summoned up courage enough to speak to her, She answered politely, always serious, never laughing with him and never permitting him to enter her house. But as he was a little conceited like all other men, he fancied that her face became a little rosier than usual when she conversed with him.

But a reputation once ruined is so hard to build up again, and always remains so fragile, that in spite of all La

Blanchette's shadowy reserve, people were already talking about her.

As for Simon, he loved his new papa very much, and took a walk with him almost every evening when the day's work was over. He went very regularly to school and remained very dignified among his comrades, never answering them.

Nevertheless one day the boy who had first annoyed him, said to him:

"You have lied! You have no papa called Philip."

"Why?" asked Simon, very much affected.

The big boy rubbed his hands together dubiously, then he said:

"Because if you had one he would be your mamma's husband."

Simon felt worried by the force of this argument, but he replied:

"He is my papa all the same."

"Oh, that might be," answered the lad with a sneering laugh, "but he is not a real papa after all."

La Blanchette's little one walked off with his eyes fixed on the ground, until he came to Father Loizon's forge, where Philip was working.

The forge was almost buried under the trees. It was very dark there; only the red light of a forge-fire threw its flickering light upon five blacksmiths, who with arms all bare hammered upon their anvils with a terrible noise. They stood erect, illuminated by fire like demons, with eyes fixed upon the burning iron they were torturing; and their heavy thoughts rose and fell with their hammers.

Simon entered unperceived, and pulled his friend very gently by the sleeve. He turned round, suddenly the work stopped, and all the men looked, very attentively. Then in the midst of this unaccustomed silence, the little thin voice of Simon was heard.

"Say, Philip, Michaude's boy just told me that you were not really my papa."

"How is that?" asked the mechanic.

"Because you are not the husband of my mamma."

Nobody laughed. Philip remained standing, leaning his forehead upon the backs of his broad hands which were resting upon the handle of his hammer, standing upon the anvil. He was thinking. His four comrades looked at him; but Simon, a tiny figure among these five giants, waited anxiously. Suddenly one of the smiths, uttering the thought of the rest, said to Philip:

"I don't care!—that La Blanchette is a brave, good girl all the same, and hard working and well behaved in spite of her misfortunes, and would make a splendid wife for a good man."

"That is true," said the other three.

The workman continued:

"And is it her fault, poor girl! if she made a mistake? She was promised marriage, and I know of more than one who is called respectable to-day, who did as bad!"

"That's true," chimed in the others in chorus. He continued: "Yes, and what she has done and how she has worked and stinted herself, and how much she has cried since she stopped going out anywhere except to church—only the good God above us knows."

"That's true again," said the others.

And then nothing was heard save the panting of the bellows beating fresh life into the dying forge-fire. Philip suddenly leaned down over Simon.

"Go tell your mamma that I want to speak to her this evening!"

Then he took the child by the shoulders and pushed him gently out of the forge.

He returned to his work and forthwith the five hammers fell altogether upon the anvils. They battered the glowing iron until night, strong, mighty, joyous, like well-satisfied hammers. But just as the great bell of a cathedral on holy days makes its diapason heard above the chiming of all other bells, so the hammer of Philip dominating the thunder of the rest, came down, second after second, with a strong sound. And he forged passionately with glowing eyes and a fountain of sparks about him.

The sky was full of stars when he knocked at the door of La Blanchette's house. He had on his Sunday blouse, a clean shirt and a neatly trimmed beard. The young woman came to the door and said to him with a sad look:

"It is wrong to come, Monsieur Philip, after dark."

He tried to answer, stammered, and remained confused before her.

She continued: "You know perfectly well, nevertheless, that I cannot allow people to have any reason to talk badly about me."

Then he suddenly cried:

"What need you care if you will only be my wife?"

No voice answered him, but he thought he heard in the darkness the sound of a body falling.

He rushed in, and Simon lying in his little bed, caught the sound of a kiss, and heard his mother murmuring something in a low sweet voice. Then suddenly the child felt himself lifted out of bed in the arms of his friend, and the smith holding him out at full length of his herculean arms cried:

"You can tell your school-fellows that your papa is Philip Remy, the smith, and that he will pull the ears of anybody who hurts you."

Next day, just as school was beginning, and all the scholars had taken their places, little Simon arose, and with pale and trembling lips but clear voice, said:

"My papa is Philip Remy, the blacksmith, and he has promised to pull the ears of anybody who hurts me."

This time nobody laughed; for everybody knew him well, that splendid Philip Remy, and he was indeed a papa of whom anybody might have been proud.

A MADMAN

A MADMAN
(From *Monsieur Parent*.)

HE died judge of a high tribunal,—an upright magistrate whose irreproachability of life was cited in all the courts of France. Attorneys, young barristers, and even judges had been wont to bow very low as a special mark of profound respect, whenever they saluted his great white meagre face, illuminated by two brilliant and deep-set eyes.

He had passed his whole life in the prosecution of crime and the protection of the weak. Thieves and murderers had no enemy more terrible than he; for he seemed to read their secret thoughts in the very depths of their souls; and to unravel, with a single look, all the mysteries of their plots.

So he died at the age of eighty-two, an object of universal homage, followed to his grave by the regrets of an entire people. Soldiers in red trousers escorted him to the tomb; and men in white cravats had poured out upon his coffin many phrases of grief and many tears that appeared to be sincere.

Now, this is the extraordinary document which an astonished notary discovered in the Judge's writing desk,—the same desk in which he was accustomed to preserve all the papers relating to important criminal cases.

It bore this simple title:

WHY?

20th June, 1851.—I have just left the court-room. I sentenced Blondel to death! Why on earth did that man kill his five children? Why? . . . People are often to be met with who find a delight in destroying life. Yes, yes, it must be a pleasure,—the greatest of all pleasures, perhaps; for killing is the nearest thing to creating, is it not? To make, to destroy! These two words include the history of the universe, all the history of all worlds, all that exists—all! Why is it intoxicating to kill?

25th June.—To think that a creature is there—a creature that lives, that walks, that runs. . . . A creature? What is a creature? a being? That animated thing, having within it the principle of movement and a will governing that movement! That thing depends on nothing. Its feet do not communicate with the soil. It is an atom of life that moves upon the earth; and that atom of life, come from I know not whence, can be destroyed at will. Then nothing, absolutely nothing. The thing rots; that is the end of it.

26th June.—Why is it a crime to kill?—Yes, why is it? On the contrary to kill is a law of nature. The mission of every being is to kill;—he kills in order to live, and he also kills for the sake of killing. . . . To kill is a part of our nature;—killing is absolutely necessary. The animal kills unceasingly, all day long, at every instant of its existence. Man kills unceasingly for the sake of food; but as he is under the necessity of also killing for sport, he invented hunting! The child kills any insects he happens to find,—little birds,—any little animals that happen to fall into his hands. But even all this does not satisfy the irresistible necessity of massacre that is born within us. It is not enough to kill dumb brutes; we need also to kill men. In ancient times this need was satisfied by human sacrifices. To-day the necessities of social existence have made murder a crime. The assassin is condemned and punished! But as we cannot live without yielding to this natural and imperious instinct of slaughter, we find relief occasionally in wars, during which one whole nation slaughters another whole nation. Then we have an orgy of blood,—a debauch which maddens armies and intoxicates even the *bourgeois,* and the women, and the children who read the exciting recital of massacres by the light of the evening lamp.

And it might be supposed that those destined to execute such human butcheries are despised! No: Honours are lavished upon them! They are garbed in gold and brilliantly coloured cloth; their heads are bedecked with plumes, their breasts with decorations; and they receive crosses, rewards, titles of every description. They are proud, respected, beloved by women, cheered by crowds,—simply because it is their mission to shed human blood. They drag through all our streets their implements of death, which the black-clad passers-by look at with envy. For to kill is the great law implanted by nature in the heart of every being! There is nothing so fine, so honourable, as to kill!

30*th June.*—To kill is the law, because Nature loves eternal youth. She seems to cry out through all her unconscious acts: *"Quick! quick! quick!"* The more she destroys, the more she renews herself.

2*d July.*—The being—what is the being? Everything and nothing. By thought he is the reflection of all things. By memory and science he is an epitome of that world whereof he hears the history within him. A mirror of objects,—a mirror of facts,—each human being becomes a miniature universe in the midst of the universe.

But travel; look upon the swarming of races;—and the man is no longer anything!—he is nothing, absolutely nothing! Go on board of a ship, and sail away from that shore which is so thronged with people, and you will soon be able to perceive nothing but the shore itself. So little, so insignificant is the individual, the imperceptible being, that he disappears utterly. Traverse Europe by rail, and look out of the car-window as you travel. Men, men, always men—innumerable, unknown,—swarming in the fields, swarming in the streets;—stupid peasants with barely enough sense to enable them to till the ground,—hideous women, knowing just enough to be able to make soup for the males and to bear children. Go to India, go to China; and again you will see the movement of thousands of millions of beings that are born, that live, and that finally die without leaving any more trace of their existence on the face of the world than the ant that is crushed upon some highroad. Go to the country of the blacks, huddling in their huts of mud; or go to the land of the whiter Arabs, sheltered by some brown tent flapping in the wind;—and you will comprehend that the individual, the single being, considered apart, is nothing, nothing at all. The race is everything. What is one being?—what is one member of one wandering tribe of the desert? Among those men of the desert, who are wise, death is never a subject of anxiety. The man is not taken into consideration. One kills one's enemy: that is war. Long ago the same things were done among our people,—it was war between house and house, between province and province.

3rd July.—It must be a strange and savoury pleasure to kill; to have right before you some living, thinking being,— to make a little hole in that being, just only one little hole, —to see the flowing of that red thing called blood, which makes life,—and then to find you have nothing before you but a mass of soft, cold, inert flesh, empty of thought!

5th August.—I who have passed all my life in judging people, in sentencing them, in killing by mere word of mouth, in killing with the guillotine those who have killed with the knife,—I!—I!—were I to do as the assassins I have sentenced,—I!—I!—who could ever know it?

10th August.—Who could ever find it out?   Could anyone suspect me—me!—me!—especially if I should select an individual whose existence I would have no personal motive in suppressing?

15th August.—The temptation!   Temptation has entered into me like a crawling worm.   It crawls; it advances; it creeps through all my body,—through all my mind also, my mind which now dwells only upon this one idea, *kill*:—it has entered my eyes which want to see blood, to see the act of dying; it has entered my ears which perpetually ring with an unfamiliar, hideous, agonizing, maddening sound, like the last outcry of a creature; it has entered into my feet, which tremble with the desire to go, to go to the spot where the act shall be done;—it is in my hands which quiver with the longing to slay.   How agreeable it must be!—how refined!— how well worthy of a free man, superior to other men, master of his own heart, and ever thirsting for new and exquisite sensations!

Yes; wander over the world and watch the swarming of men—innumerable, unknown men.   *Unknown?* Ah! there is the key to the whole enigma.   To kill is criminal because we have counted the number of creatures!   When one of them is born, the fact is registered;—the creature is named, is baptized.   The law claims possession of all these!   There's the secret!   But the being that is not registered does not count! Kill such a one wherever you find him,—on the heath or in the desert, on the mountain or upon the plain,—it matters not! Nature loves death! She never punishes the slayer!

What is particularly sacred, by the way, is the civil state! You understand! The individual is sacred because he is registered as belonging to the civil state! Respect the civil state — the legal God! On your knees!

The government can kill, because it possesses the power to modify the civil condition. When it causes two hundred thousand men to be slaughtered in war, it erases them all from its civil register, it suppresses them by the hand of its recorders. And that is the end of the matter. But the rest of us,—we who have no power to change the records of municipalities,— we are obliged to respect life. Civil state, glorious Divinity who reignest in the temples of municipalities, I bow before thee! Thou art stronger than Nature is. Ah! ah!

22d August.—I could not resist any longer. I have just killed a little creature as an experiment,—as a commencement.

My servant Jean had a goldfinch, which he used to keep in a cage hanging at the office window. I sent him out on an errand; and then I took the little bird in my hand—in my hand, against which I could feel his heart beat. He was quite warm. I went up to my room. From time to time I squeezed him a little harder—then his heart beat more quickly: it was a sensation at once atrocious and delicious. I was very nearly on the point of smothering him. But if I had smothered him, I would not have seen the blood.

Then I took a pair of scissors,—short-bladed nail scissors; and I cut his throat with three nips—very slowly. He opened his beak, he tried to escape; but I held him—oh! I held him! —I could have held an enraged mastiff! and I saw the blood come. How beautiful blood is!—red, shining, bright! I wanted to drink it. I dipped the end of my tongue into it! It is good. But then he had so little of it—that poor atom of a bird! I did not have time enough to enjoy the sight as I would have liked to do. It must be simply superb to see a bull bleed.

And then I did just as the murderers do—real murderers. I washed the scissors; I washed my hands; I threw the water away; and I took the body, the corpse, into the garden to bury it. I hid it under a strawberry plant. It will never be found there. Every day I intend to eat one strawberry off that plant. How one can really enjoy life . . . when he knows how!

My servant cried. He thought his bird had flown away. How could he ever suspect me! Ah! ah!

25th August.—I must really kill a man! It must be done.

30th August.—It has been done. How easy a thing to do!

I had gone out to the Bois de Vernes just for a walk. I was not thinking about anything in particular,—not thinking about anything at all. A child came along the pathway—a little boy eating a slice of bread and butter.

He stopped to watch me pass by, and said: "Good-day, your Honour!"

Then the thought came into my head: *Suppose I kill him?* . . .

I replied:

"Well, my boy, are you all by yourself?"

"Yes, sir."

"All by yourself in the woods, eh?"

"Yes, sir."

And the wish to kill him made me drunk like alcohol. I approached him very gently, being afraid that he might try to run away. And all of a sudden I seized him by the throat. . . . And I squeezed his throat; I squeezed it. I squeezed it with all my might. He looked at me with such a frightful look in his eyes! What eyes! Big, and all round,—deep, limpid, terrible! Never did I experience an emotion so brutal . . . yet so brief! He tried to pull my wrists with his little hands; and his body twisted like a feather flung upon hot coals. Finally he ceased to move at all.

My heart beat so fast—ah! I thought of the heart of the bird! I threw the body into the ditch; and put some grass over it. . . .

I went home. I ate a hearty dinner. How easily the thing is done! I was very merry that evening,—quite jovial; felt ever so much younger. I passed the evening at the house of the Prefect of Police. Everybody thought I was unusually witty.

30th August.—The corpse has been found. The police are looking for the murderer. Ah! ah!

1st September.—Two tramps have been arrested. No proofs against them.

2d September.—The parents of the boy came to see me. They wept!—oh! how they wept. Ah! ah!

6th October.—No clew whatever has been found. It is supposed that some tramp must have done the deed. Ah! ah! If I could only have had the pleasure of seeing the blood actually flow, I think I should now feel perfectly satisfied!

10th October.—The desire to kill thrills the very marrow of my bones. It is a desire comparable for intensity to nothing except the passion of love at twenty years.

20th October.—Still another. I was taking a walk on the river bank, after breakfast. And I saw a fisherman sleeping under a willow tree. It was mid-day. A spade seemed to have been left on purpose sticking in the clay of a neighbouring potato field.

I took it;—I came back;—I lifted it like a club; and with the edge of it, I split the fisherman's head at one blow. Oh!— but he bled—that one! Pink blood, full of brains. It trickled into the river very gently. And I walked away with a solemn step. Suppose anybody had seen me! . . . Ah! ah! I would have made an excellent murderer.

25th October.—The murder of the fisherman has caused a great excitement. His nephew, who was fishing with him, is accused of the murder.

26th October.—The examining judge declares that the nephew is guilty. Everybody in town believes it. Ah! ah!

27th October.—The nephew's defence is very poor indeed. He says that he went to the village to buy some bread and cheese. He swears that his uncle must have been killed while he was away! Who is going to believe him?

28th October.—The nephew has almost been forced to confess; they have confused him so! Ah! ah! This is justice!

15th November.—The evidence against the nephew is overwhelming. It appears that he was to inherit his uncle's property. I am to try the case!

25th January.—To death! to death! to death! I have sentenced him to death! Ah! ah! The prosecuting attorney argued like an angel! Ah! ah! Still another. I will go to see the execution.

10th March.—It is all over. He is dead now, sure enough— dead as a door nail! I enjoyed it immensely! How beautiful it is to see a man's head chopped off! The blood gushed out like a stream—like a torrent! Oh! if I had been able, how I should have liked to bathe in it! What delight to lie down in it,—to get the warm jet right in my face, and in my hair,—and to get up all red, all red! Ah! if they only knew!

Now I shall wait. I can afford to wait. It would require so little to betray me. . . .

The MS. contained many more pages, but no reference to any new crime.

The medical alienists to whom it was confided declare that many unknown madmen exist in society—quite as adroit and quite as terrible as this demented monster.

SOLITUDE

SOLITUDE

(From *Monsieur Parent.*)

IT was after a bachelor's dinner. The party had been very merry. One of the guests,—an old friend,—asked me:

"Will you walk home with me by the Avenue des Champs-Elysées?"

And we started down the long promenade, walking slowly, under the trees which were as yet scarcely clad with their spring foliage. No noise, except that vague and everlasting murmur that Paris makes. A cool wind breathed in our faces; and the legion of the stars sprinkled the black sky with dust of gold.

My companion said:

"I cannot tell why, but I can breathe freer here at night than anywhere else. It seems that my thoughts become larger here. At times there come to my mind those singular gleams which make a man think for a second that he has discovered the divine secret of things. Then the window closes again! That is the end of it."

At intervals we could see a pair of shadows gliding along the line of trees;—or we would pass by a bench where two beings, seated side by side, made a single silhouette against the night.

My companion muttered:

47

"Poor things! They do not inspire me with contempt, but with an immense pity. Among all the mysteries of human life, there is just one that I have been able to penetrate. It is this,—that our whole suffering in life comes from the fact that we are eternally alone, and that all our efforts, all our actions, are inspired by the desire to escape from this solitude. Those folks there—those lovers sitting on benches in the open air,—are simply trying like ourselves, and like all living creatures, to get rid of their isolation,—even if it is only for a minute. But they remain,—they will remain always alone, and we also.

"We can perceive each other more or less; we can do nothing more.

"For a long time I have endured this abominable torture—the torture of having been able to learn, to discover the frightful solitude in which I live—and I know that nothing can change that solitude—nothing, do you understand?

"Whatever we strive to do, whatever we manage to accomplish, whatever be the aspiration of our hearts, the appeal of our lips, the embrace of our arms, we remain always alone.

"I asked you to take this walk with me to-night, so that I might not be obliged to go home, because I suffer horribly now from the loneliness of my lodgings. What good will it do me, I wonder? Now I am speaking to you; you are listening to me; and still we are both of us alone—side by side, but still alone. Do you understand me?

" 'Blessed are the poor in spirit,' says the Scripture. They

SOLITUDE

have the delusion of happiness. Those people do not feel
our miserable solitude. They do not wander through life, as I
do, feeling no other contact but that of elbows—no other joy
than the selfish satisfaction of comprehending, seeing, divining
and eternally suffering from the knowledge of our endless
isolation.

"You think I am slightly crazy, don't you?

"Listen to me! Ever since I first felt the solitude of my
existence, it has seemed to me that I advance each day, further
and further, into some dark subterranean place, whose sides
I cannot feel, whose end I do not know, and which, perhaps,
is without end! I advance without any companion, without
any one near me, without feeling that any other living being
is following the same shadowy path. That subterranean way
is *Life*. Sometimes I hear sounds—voices, cries. . . . I grope
my way toward those vague noises. But I never know exactly
from whence they come; I never met a soul; I never feel
another hand in the blackness that surrounds me. Do you
understand me?

"Some other men have also divined this atrocious suffering.
"Musset cried out:

'Who comes? Who calls me? None.
I am alone.—'Tis the hour that strikes—
O solitude! O wretchedness!'

"But with him, it was only a passing doubt,—not a positive
certitude, as it is with me. He was a poet;—he peopled his

life with phantoms, with dreams. He was never truly alone.
I—I am alone!

"Gustave Flaubert, one of the greatest of unhappy men of
this age, because he was also one of the most lucid, wrote
to a woman-friend this despairing phrase: 'We all live in a
desert. No one person understands any other person.'

"No;—no one understands anybody,—no matter what may
be thought, or said, or tried. Does the Earth herself understand what is going on among those stars up there,—scattered
like seeds of fire through space,—so far away that we can
discern the light of a few only, while the innumerable multi-
tudes of the others is lost in the infinite,—and nevertheless
so relatively near to each other that they may form one
whole, like the molecules of a body?

"Well, a man knows just as little concerning what is going
on in the mind of another man. We are still further away
from each other than those stars,—we are, above all, more
isolated, because thought is unfathomable.

"Can you imagine anything more frightful than this continual brushing-past-us of creatures impenetrable by our
thought! We love as if we were enchained,—close, close,—
our arms held out to embrace; yet we can never be united.
A torturing thirst for union consumes us; but all our efforts
remain sterile.—our self-abandonments fruitless, our confi-
dences useless, our caresses impotent, our embraces vain.
When we wish to mingle together, our rush to each other only
results in bruising ourselves against each other.

"I never feel more utterly alone than when I open my heart to some friend, because it is then that I best understand the insurmountable barrier between us. He is there before me— that man;—I see his clear eyes upon me! but his soul, the something that is behind those eyes,—I know nothing about it. He is listening to me. But what is he thinking? Yes, what is he thinking? You do not understand that torment? He hates me, perhaps?—or despises me?—or secretly mocks me,—eh? He reflects upon what I say; he judges me; he rails at me; he condemns me; he holds me to be tiresome or stupid. How find out what he thinks? How know if he loves me as I love him?—how know what is going on in that little round head? What greater mystery than the secret thought of a fellow-being?—the hidden and absolutely free thought, which we can neither know, nor master, nor drive, nor conquer?

"And I,—in vain have I striven to give myself wholly to another,—to open all the gates of my soul: never can I yield myself up. I keep within, at the very centre of my being,— that sanctuary of the *Ego* into which none can enter. Nobody can discover it, nobody can look into it,—because nobody else is exactly like me,—because nobody understands anybody.

"Do you yourself even understand me at this moment? No, you think I am mad! You are watching me—you are on your guard against me! You are saying to yourself: 'What has got into him to-night?' But if, some future day or other, you should find yourself able to fully divine, to fully grasp the nature of my horrible and subtle suffering,—then come at

least and say to me: '*I have understood you!*'—and you will
make me happy, for a second, perhaps.

"But women especially cause me to perceive my solitude.

"Misery! misery! How much I have suffered through them,
because they have often,—much more often than men,—given
me the illusion of not being really alone!

"When one enters into the domain of Love, one seems to
grow larger. A superhuman felicity fills your being. But do
you know why? Do you know the reason of that vast sensation of happiness? It is simply and solely because one then
imagines he is no longer alone. The isolation, the abandonment of the human creature appears to cease. Oh! what an
error!

"Woman, woman, far more tortured than we men are by
that eternal need of love which gnaws our lonesome hearts—
woman is the great Lie of the Dream.

"You have known the deliciousness of those hours we pass
face to face with that long-haired being, whose features
bewitch, whose look makes us delirious. What madness then
deludes us! What illusion carries us away!

"She and I, we are to become one, it seems, by-and-by?
But that by-and-by never comes, and after long weeks of waiting, of hoping, of deceitful joy, the day comes when I suddenly
find myself much more alone than I ever was before.

"After each kiss, each embrace,—the isolation becomes
vaster. And how torturing it is, how frightful! . . .

"And then, adieu! It is all over. After a while one scarcely recognizes the woman who had been everything to us for one moment of our lives, and whose secret thought we have never been able to read,—a thought, commonplace enough, no doubt, if one could know it.

"Even in those hours when it would seem that in the mysterious accord of two beings,—in the complete intermingling of all desires and aspirations,—one could descend into the very depth of another's soul,—one word, one single word, reveals to us our error, and betrays, as a lightning-flash in the night, the black and unfathomable gulf between us.

"And nevertheless, the best thing in all this world is to pass an evening with the woman you love,—without speaking at all,—feeling almost perfectly happy in the simple feeling that she is there. Never ask for anything more than this joy; for two beings can never mix together.

"As for myself, I have now closed the door of my heart. I no longer allow myself to tell any one what I believe, what I think, or what I love. Knowing myself forever condemned to hideous solitude, I observe things without ever giving my opinion. What matter to me opinions, disputes, pleasures, beliefs? Being unable to share anything with anybody, I have become indifferent to everything. My invisible thought remains unexplored. I always have certain commonplace phrases ready as answers to the questions addressed to me every day, and a smile that means 'Yes,' when I will not even take the trouble to speak.

"Do you understand me?"

*   *   *   *   *   *   *

We had ascended the Avenue again as far as the Arc de Triomphe; then we had retraced our steps, back to the Place de la Concorde;—for he had said all these things very slowly, together with many other things which I cannot now remember.

He stopped; and, suddenly extending his arm toward the lofty obelisk of granite,—(towering above the Paris pavement, to lose its long Egyptian profile among the stars),—a monument in exile, bearing on its flank in strange graven signs the history of its country,—my friend cried out:

"See! we are all like that stone!"

Then he left me without another word.

Was he drunk? Was he crazy? Was he speaking the truth? I do not yet know. Sometimes I think he was right;—then again it seems to me that he must have lost his reason.

THE HAND

THE HAND

. . . I WAS at one time police magistrate in Ajaccio,—a little white city, which sleeps at the edge of an admirable gulf, shut in by lofty mountains.

The cases I had to investigate or prosecute there, were mostly cases of vendetta. In Corsloa there are all sorts of vendettas,—superb and dramatic as possible,—some ferocious, others heroic. You can study there the finest themes of vengeance possible to dream about;—hatreds that are centuries old, appeased for a moment, but never totally extinguished,— abominable ruses,—murders that have the extent of massacres, and sometimes of a character almost resembling a glorious act. For two years I was always hearing about blood-money, and about that terrible Corsican prejudice which compels one to revenge an injury on the person who inflicted it,—upon his descendants and upon his relatives. I saw old men, children, and remote cousins murdered; and my head was full of all such stories.

Well, one day I was told that an Englishman had just leased for several years in advance a little country-house that stood at the innermost point of the gulf. He had brought with him a French servant, whom he hired at Marseilles, on his way to Corsica.

In a short time everybody was talking about this strange person, who lived by himself,—never leaving his house except to hunt or fish. He never spoke to anybody and never went to the city; but every morning he used to practise shooting for an hour or two, with a pistol or a carbine.

All kinds of stories began to circulate about him. Some said he was a very distinguished nobleman, who had left his country for political reasons;—others said he was trying to hide himself because he had committed some terrible crime. Various peculiarly horrible circumstances were related in connection with the legend.

In my quality of police magistrate I thought it necessary to try and obtain some particulars about the man; but I found it impossible to get any information. He called himself Sir John Rowell.

I contented myself, therefore, with having a close watch set over him; but none of my men could find anything very suspicious in his actions.

After a time, as the queer rumors about him continued, and increased, and became general, I resolved to see the stranger for myself; and I made a point of going out hunting every day in the neighbourhood of his place.

I had to wait a long time for a chance. It came at last in the shape of a partridge which I brought down under the very nose of my Englishman. My dog brought it to me; but, taking the bird in my hand, I went to Sir John Rowell's, to excuse myself and beg him to accept the game.

He was a very tall man with red hair and a red beard—
very tall indeed, and also very broad,—a sort of placid and
polite Hercules. He had nothing of the ordinary British stiff-
ness about him, and he thanked me warmly for my courtesy
in the peculiarly accented French of our cousins across the
Channel. During the following month we had five or six
meetings and brief conversations.

One evening at last, as I was passing by his gate, I saw
him in his garden, bestraddling a chair and smoking a pipe.
I saluted him, and he invited me in to take a glass of ale.
I was only too glad to accept.

He received me with all the minute English courtesy possible, and spoke warmly of France and of Corsica,—declaring
that he loved the country and the Gulf shore. He per-
sistently said *cette* when he ought to have said *ce*.

Then, with the greatest precaution, I began to question
him—disguising my object under the mask of a warm personal interest—about his life and his projects. He replied
without the least embarrassment, and told me that he had
travelled a great deal—in Africa, in India, in America. He
added, laughing, in bad French:

"Adventures?—yes; I have had plenty of adventures. Oh!
yes!"

I turned the conversation upon hunting; and he began to
give me the most curious facts about hippopotamus hunting
and tiger hunting and elephant hunting and even gorilla
hunting.

I said:

"But all those are terribly dangerous animals."

He smiled and said:

"Oh! no—the worst of all is Man."

Then he burst into a laugh—a big, hearty, self-satisfied English laugh and observed:

"I've done a good deal of Man-hunting, too, in my time."

Then he began to talk about weapons, and invited me into a room to show me his firearms, and explain the difference in their mechanism.

His parlour was all hung in black—black silk embroidered in gold. Huge bright-yellow flowers blossomed all over the sable texture,—shining like fire.

"That," he observed, "is Japanese work."

But in the centre of the largest panel there was a strange thing which caught my eye,—a black object relieved against a square of red velvet. I approached it:—it was a hand— a man's hand. Not a skeleton hand, all white and clean, but a hand black and desiccated,—with the yellow nails, the naked muscles, and traces of blood—blood like a scab—upon the bones at the point where they had been severed, as with the blow of an ax, about the middle of the forearm.

Round the wrist an enormous chain of iron had been riven about the foul relic; and this chain fastened the hand to the wall by a great ring solid enough to hold an elephant in leash.

I asked:

"What is that?"

The Englishman tranquilly answered:

"That was part of my best enemy. It is from America. It was cut off with a sabre, and the skin removed with a sharp stone,—after which it was dried in the sun for eight days. That was a good thing for me, I tell you!"

I touched that fragment of human wreck, which seemed to have belonged to a colossus. The fingers, extraordinarily long, were attached to enormous tendons, still held in their places here and there by strips of skin. Flayed as it was, that hand was something hideous;—it made one think involuntarily of some savage vengeance.

I said:

"That man must have been very strong."

The Englishman answered gently:

"Oh, yes; but I was stronger than he. . . . I put this chain on the hand to hold it."

I thought he was joking. I said:

"But the chain is no use now. The hand can't get away."

Sir John Rowell gravely answered:

"That hand always tries to get away. The chain is necessary."

I glanced quickly at his face, thinking to myself: "Is he mad, or is he trying to make a stupid joke!"

But his face remained impenetrable,—tranquil and good natured. I turned the conversation to another subject, and began to look at the rifles.

Meanwhile I observed that three loaded revolvers were lying upon different articles of furniture,—as if the man was living in perpetual fear of being attacked.

I went to see him two or three times afterward. Then I did not go any more. People had become accustomed to his presence: and he was absolutely indifferent to the rest of the world.

*   *   *   *   *   *   *

A whole year passed. Then, one morning, about the end of November, my servant woke me up with the news that Sir John Rowell had been murdered during the night.

Half an hour later I entered the Englishman's house, with the central commissary and the captain of the gendarmes. The French valet was weeping at the door, terrified and inconsolable. I first suspected him; but the man subsequently proved to be innocent.

The real murderer was never known.

The first sight that met my eyes on entering the parlour was the corpse of Sir John Rowell,—lying on its back, in the middle of the room.

His vest was torn, one shirt-sleeve, half pulled off, was hanging down;—everything indicated that an awful struggle had taken place.

The Englishman had been strangled to death! His blackened and swollen face, frightfully distorted, were an expression of hideous fear; between his clenched teeth was a bit of something or other, which I could not tell the nature of at first; and his throat, pierced with five wounds that seemed to have been made by points of iron, was covered with blood.

A doctor joined us. He examined the marks of the fingers in the flesh for a long time, and then uttered these strange words:

"Why, the man looks as if he had been strangled by a skeleton!"

I felt a creeping sensation; and involuntarily lifted my eyes to the wall—to the place where the horrible flayed hand used to be. It was no longer there. The chain—broken—was dangling from the ring.

Then I bent over the dead man, and between his clenched teeth I found one of the fingers of the vanished hand,—severed, or rather sawed off by the teeth, about the middle of the second joint. . . .

Then we proceeded to take testimony. We could not find out anything at all. No door had been broken in,—no window, no partition. Even the two watchdogs had never been awakened.

The testimony of the servant was, in substance, about as follows:

For a month previously his master had seemed to be very much worried about something. He had received a great many letters, which he burned as soon as he had read them.

Frequently he would fly into a rage that seemed like madness, and, taking a whip, would lash the dried hand furiously—the same hand that had been removed from its place

on the wall in some mysterious way, at the time of the
murder.

Sir John used to go to bed very late, and always locked
himself in carefully. He never slept without having pistols
or loaded revolvers within arm's reach. Often, in the night,
he used to shout out very loud, as if he was quarrelling with
somebody.

That night, by some singular chance, he had made no noise
at all; and the valet had only found that Sir John was murdered when he went to open the windows next morning. He
did not know whom to suspect. . . .

I communicated all the information I possessed concerning the man to the other magistrates and police officials; and
the most rigorous search was made in all parts of the island.
Nothing whatever was discovered. . . .

. . . Now, one night,—three months after the crime, I had
a hideous nightmare. I thought I saw the Hand,—the horrible Hand,—running like a scorpion or a spider along the
curtains and up and down the walls of my room. Three
times I woke up;—three times I went to sleep again; three
times I saw the ghastly thing running all over my room, and
using its fingers like so many legs.

Next day they brought me the Hand itself,—saying they
had found it in the cemetery, and on the tomb of Sir John
Rowell, who had been buried there; for we never could find
the address of his family. . . . *The index finger was wanting.*

That is my story, ladies;—and that is all I know about it.

* * * * * * *

. . . All the women had turned pale;—some shuddered visibly. One cried out:

"But that is no ending of a story;—there is no explanation! We shall not be able to sleep to-night if you do not tell us what really happened—or, at least, what you think really happened."

The magistrate smiled austerely.

"Oh! as for my opinion, ladies,—it will certainly dissipate your terrible fancies. I merely suppose that the legitimate proprietor of that hand was not dead, and that he came back with his other hand to look for it. But how he managed to fulfill his purpose is something, I must acknowledge, which I have never been able to surmise. . . . It was, of course, a sort of vendetta."

One of the women murmured:

"No; it could never be . . . !"

The police Judge, still smiling, observed:

"I told you so!—I knew that my explanation would not satisfy you. . . ."

'TOINE

'TOINE

I

EVERYBODY for ten leagues round knew old 'Toine, "Big 'Toine," 'Toine-*Ma-Fine,* Antoine Mâcheblé, also nicknamed Brulot,—the tavern-keeper of Tournevent.

He had given celebrity to that little hamlet, hidden in a wrinkle of the valley which sloped down to the sea—a poor little peasant-village composed of ten Normandy cottages surrounded by ditches and trees.

They stood,—all those houses—as if trying to shrink out of sight among the tall grass and reeds of the ravine,—behind the curve which had given the place its name,—*Tournevent.* They seemed to have hunted for this shelter for themselves, just as those birds that hide in plowed furrows on days of tempest seek to shelter themselves from the great wind of the sea, the ocean-wind,—rough and salty—which gnaws and burns like fire, which dries up and destroys like the winter frosts.

But the entire hamlet seemed to be the property of Antoine Mâcheblé, nicknamed Brulot, also very often called 'Toine, and 'Toine-Ma-Fine, because of a certain phrase that was forever in his mouth:

"My *fine* is the best in all France."

His *fine* was his cognac, let it be understood.

For twenty years he had been slaking the thirst of the country with his *fine* and his *brûlots;* for whenever anybody would ask him:

"What had I better take, Father Antoine?"

He invariably responded:

"A burnt brandy, son-in-law;—it warms up the tripes and clears up the head;—nothing better for the inside!"

He also had the habit of calling everyone "son-in-law"—although he never had a married daughter, nor even a daughter to marry.

Yes, indeed! everybody knew 'Toine Brulot, the biggest man in the canton, and even in the whole *arrondissement.* His little house seemed ridiculously too narrow and too low to contain him; and when you saw him standing at his door, as he would do for a whole day at a time, you could not have helped wondering how he would ever manage to get inside again. But inside he would get—somehow or other—every time a customer came; for it was 'Toine's acknowledged right to levy a treat upon every one who drank in his house.

The name of his tavern, painted upon the sign was *"Au Rendez-vous des Anis";* and a good name it was, seeing that Father 'Toine was the friend, sure enough, of everybody in the whole country. Folks came from Fécamp and from Montivillers to see him and to joke with him and to listen to his talk; for that big fat old fellow could have made a

tombstone laugh. He had a way of his own of joking at
folks without making them mad,—a way of winking his eye
to express what he never said,—a way of slapping his own
thigh when he got to laughing, so funny that at every slap
he was bound to make you also laugh with him, whether
you wanted to or not. And then it was good fun only just
to see him drink. He would drink every time anybody asked
him, and drink everything offered him,—with a look of joy
in his mischievous eye—a joy of twofold origin, inspired
first by the pleasure of being treated, and secondly by the
delight of piling away so many big coppers paid down as
the price of the fun.

The jokers of the neighbourhood used to say to him:

"Why don't you drink up the sea, Pap 'Toine?"

He would answer:

"There's two things prevent me—first thing is that it's
salty, and then besides it would have to be bottled, because
my abdomen isn't elastic enough for me to trust myself to
drink out of such a cup as that."

And then you ought to have heard him quarrelling with
his wife! It was better than a play! Every single day during the whole thirty years they had been married they used
to fight regularly. Only 'Toine would just joke, while his
wife would get really mad. She was a tall peasant woman,
who walked with great long steps like a crane,—and whose
slabsided, skinny body supported a head that looked like
the head of a mad owl. She spent her whole time in raising

chickens in a little backyard behind the tavern; and she was renowned for her skill in fattening fowl.

Whenever they gave a big dinner at Fécamp, up the coast, it was always considered essential to eat one of Mother 'Toine's boarders,—otherwise it would be no dinner at all.

But she had been born in a bad humour, and she had remained all her life cross with everything and everybody. And while she was ill-humoured with the world in general, she was particularly ill-humoured with her husband. She was mad at him for his good humour, for his renown, for his good health, and for his fatness. She called him a good-for-nothing, because he was able to make money without doing anything;—she called him a hog, because he ate and drank as much as ten ordinary men;—and she never passed a day of her life without declaring:

"Wouldn't he look better in the pig-pen, a beggar like that!—Makes my stomach sick to see the fat of him!"

And she would go and scream in his face:

"Wait!—you wait a bit! We'll see what'll happen to you!—we'll see soon enough! You'll bust like a grain-sack, you big, puffed-up good-for-nothing!"

Then 'Toine would slap his fat stomach, and laugh with all his might, and answer:

"Eh! Mother 'Toine, my old plank—you just try to fatten up your chickens like that,—you just try it on for the fun of the thing!"

And, pulling up his shirt-sleeve to show his enormous arm, he would cry:

"Now there's a wing for you, mother!—that's what you can call a wing."

And the customers would yell with delight, and thump the table with their fists, and stamp the earthen floor with their feet, and spit on the ground in the craziness of their merriment.

The furious old woman would yell again:

"Wait a bit!—you just wait a bit. . . . I know what's going to happen to you;—you'll bust like a grain sack!"

And off she would go, pursued by the laughter of the customers.

'Toine was indeed wonderful to behold,—so heavy and thick and red and puffy he had become. He was one of those enormous beings whom Death seems to select to amuse himself with,—to practise all his tricks and jokes and treacherous buffooneries upon,—so that his slow work of destruction may be rendered for once irresistibly funny. Instead of showing himself in his ordinary aspect to such a one, this rascally old Death forbears to manifest his presence in grey hairs or in withered limbs or in wrinkles or in that general crumbling down which makes folks exclaim,—"*Bigre!*—how changed he is!"—instead of thus acting, Death takes pleasure in fattening such a man, in making him monstrous and absurd, in colouring him up with red and blue, in puffing him out, in giving him an aspect of superhuman health; and all those deformities which in other beings seem pitiable or ghastly, become in his person laughable, droll, amusing.

"Wait a bit!—wait a bit!" repeated Mother 'Toine,—"we'll see what you'll come to yet!"

II

Well, it came to pass that 'Toine got a paralytic stroke. They put the colossus to bed in the little chamber behind the partition of the bar-room,—so that he could hear what the folks were saying on the other side, and could talk with his friends; for his head was all right, although his body,—the enormous body, impossible to move or to lift,— was stricken with immobility. At first it was hoped that he would be able to move his big legs again; but this hope vanished in a very short time; and 'Toine-Ma-Fine passed his days as well as his nights in bed,—the bed that was only made up once a week, with the assistance of four neighbours, who lifted out the tavern-keeper by his four limbs, while the mattress was being turned.

He kept his good humour still; but it was a different jollity from that of the old times,—more humble, more timid, —and he was childishly afraid of his wife, who kept yelping all day long:

"There!—the big hog;—there he is, the good-for-nothing, the lazy lout, the nasty drunkard! Ah! the nasty fellow, the nasty beast!"

He never answered her any more. He would only wink his right eye when her back was turned, and then turn himself over in bed—the only movement in his power to make. He called this exercise "taking a turn to the North,"—"taking a turn to the South."

His great amusement now was to listen to the gossip in the tavern, and to shout dialogues through the partition whenever he could recognize the voices of friends. He would yell:

"Hey, son-in-law!—that you, Celestin?"

And Celestin Maloisel would answer:

"That's me, Pap 'Toine. So you're on the way to gallop again, eh, you old rascal?"

'Toine-Ma-Fine would answer:

"Not to gallop,—no! not yet! But I've not lost flesh;— the old shell's solid as ever."

After awhile he began to call his most particular friends into his room; and they kept him company pleasantly enough —though it worried him a great deal to see them drinking without his being able to join. He kept saying:

"What kills me, son-in-law,—what just kills me is not being able to taste my *fine*,—*nom d'un nom*. As for the rest, I don't care a doggone,—but it just kills me to think I can't take a horn."

And the owl-face of old mother 'Toine appeared at the door. She screamed:

"Look at him!—look at him now, the lazy big lummox that has to be fed,—that has to be washed,—that has to be cleaned like an overgrown hog!"

And when the old woman was not there, a red cock would

sometimes jump up on the window, stare into the room with his little round carrion's eye, and crow sonorously. Sometimes also, one or two chickens would fly in as far as the foot of the bed, to look for crumbs.

'Toine-Ma-Fine's friends soon abandoned the barroom for the bed-room,—where they would assemble shortly after noon every day, to chat at the fat man's bedside.

Helpless as he was, that devil-of-a-joker 'Toine, he could make them all laugh still. He would have made Old Nick himself laugh,—the old humbug. There were three men in particular who came to see him every day: Celestin Maloisel, a tall lean fellow, a little crooked like the trunk of an apple-tree; Prosper Horslaville, a dried-up little man, with a nose like a ferret, mischievous and sly as a fox; and Césaire Paumelle, who never said anything himself, but had lots of fun for all that.

They used to get a plank out of the yard, place it on the edge of the bed, and they would play dominoes *pardi,*—great old games of dominoes, which would last from two o'clock until six.

But Mother 'Toine soon made herself insufferable. She could not endure to see her big fat lummox of a husband still amuse himself, and playing dominoes in bed; and whenever she saw they were going to begin a game, she would rush in furiously, knock the plank over, seize the dominoes and take them into the barroom;—declaring that it was bad enough to have to feed that great lump of tallow with-

out seeing him amuse himself just for spite,—just to torment the poor folks who had to work hard all day.

Celestin Maloisel and Césaire Paumelle would bow their
heads to the storm; but Prosper Horslaville found great fun
in teasing the old woman, in exciting her still more.

One day that she seemed more than usually exasperated,
he cried out:

"Hey, mother!—do you know what I'd do if I was in your
place—eh!"

She waited for him to explain himself, and watched his
face with her owlish eye.

He said:

"Say, that man of yours never's going to get out of bed,
and he's as warm as an oven. Well now, if I was you, I'd
set him to hatching eggs."

She stood speechless for a moment, thinking he was making fun of her,—closely watching the thin cunning face of
the peasant, who continued:

"Yes, I'd put five eggs under one arm, and five under the
other,—just the same time as I'd put them under a hen to
set on. Them things does be born of themselves. When
they'd be hatched, I'd take your old man's chicks and give
them to the hen to take care of. Tell you, mother,—that
way you'd soon have a slew of chickens running around!"

Astonished, the old woman said:

"But can that be done?"

"Can it be done? I'd like to know why it couldn't be

done. If you can hatch eggs in a warm box, why couldn't you hatch them in a bed?"

The old woman was greatly impressed by this reasoning, and she went off, more thoughtful than usual, and quite calmed down.

Eight days later she walked into 'Toine's room one morning with her apron full of eggs. And she said:

"I've just put the yellow hen in the nest with ten eggs under her. Now here's ten for you. See that you don't break them."

'Toine, completely dumbfounded, asked:

"What do you want now?"

She answered:

"I want you to hatch them,—you good-for-nothing."

He laughed at first; but when he found she was serious he got mad, he resisted, he positively objected to letting her put the eggs under his arms to be hatched.

But the old woman cried out in a passion:

"Then you shan't have a bit of grub until you take them. Now we'll see if you hatch them or not!"

'Toine got uneasy and didn't answer.

When he heard the clock strike twelve, he cried out:

"Hey, mother,—got the soup ready yet?"

The old woman screamed from the kitchen:

"Got no soup for you, you overgrown lazy lout."

He thought she was only joking, and he waited awhile;— then he begged, implored, swore, took a desperate turn to the

North and a desperate turn to the South, hammered the wall
with his fist,—but he was obliged to yield and to let her put
five eggs against his left side. Then he got his soup.

When his friends came, he looked so queer and so uneasy
that they thought he must be sick.

Then they proceeded to play the daily game. But 'Toine
seemed to find no fun in it, and he put out his hand very
slowly,—with infinite precaution.

"Got your arm tied up?" asked Horslaville.

'Toine responded:

"I've got a sort of a numbness in my shoulder."

Suddenly they heard somebody entering the barroom. They
stopped playing.

It was the mayor and the adjutant. They asked for two
glasses of *fine,* and began to chat about public affairs. As
they were talking very low, 'Toine wanted to put his ear
against the partition to hear them, and as he gave a sudden
"turn to the North," forgetting the eggs, he found himself
lying upon an omelette.

At the sound of the great oath which he swore, the old
woman rushed in, and suspecting the disaster, discovered it
with one pull at the bedclothes. At first she did nothing;—
she was too indignant, too suffocated with fury at the sight
of the yellow cataplasm smeared upon her old man's side.

Then, trembling with rage, she flung herself upon the paralytic; and began to thump him with all her might on the
stomach, just as if she was beating dirty linen at the pool.

Her fists came down alternately with a dull thud,—rapidly as the paws of a rabbit drumming.

The three friends of 'Toine laughed to split their sides,— sneezed, coughed, screeched; as the big fat man parried his wife's attacks with great caution, for fear of breaking the five eggs on the other side.

III

'Toine was vanquished. He had to hatch; he had to give up playing dominoes; he had to give up all active existence; —for the old woman ferociously cut off his rations every time he broke an egg.

So he lived upon his back, with his eyes on the ceiling— motionless,—his arms lifted up like wings,—while the chicken-germs were warmed against his sides.

He only talked in whispers, as if he were as afraid of noise as he was of motion; and he began to feel an anxious sympathy for the yellow hen that followed the same occupation as himself.

He would ask his wife:

"Did the yellow one eat last night?"

And the old woman would keep running from her husband to her chickens, and from her chickens to her husband —terribly busy with the chickens that were being hatched in the nest and in the bed.

The country folk who knew the story would come, very seriously and full of curious interest to ask after 'Toine. They would enter on tiptoe as if they were coming into a sick room, and say:

"Well, how is it?"

'Toine would answer:

"Well, it's doing good enough; but it gives me the itch to be so hot;—makes all my skin creep."

Now, one morning his wife came in, very much excited, and said:

"The yellow one has seven. There were three bad."

'Toine felt his heart beat. He wondered how many he was going to have.

He asked.

"How long before it'll happen."

The old woman would answer angrily—herself anxious through fear of a failure.

"Got to hope so."

They waited. Friends who knew the time was approaching, became anxious.

They talked about it everywhere; folks went from house to house to ask for news.

About 3 o'clock in the afternoon, 'Toine fell asleep. He had got into the habit of sleeping half the day. He was suddenly awakened by a tickling under his right arm. He put down his hand and seized a little creature covered with yellow down, which moved in his fingers.

His excitement was such that he yelled, and let go the chicken which began to run all over the bedclothes. The tavern was full of people. The customers all rushed in, and thronged in a circle as if round a mountebank's performance;

and the old woman came to carefully gather up the little bird which had hidden itself under her husband's beard.

Nobody spoke. It was a warm April day. Through the open window could be heard the clucking of the old hen, calling her chickens.

'Toine, who was sweating with excitement, constraint, and anxiety, murmured:

"I've another under the left arm,—right now!"

His wife plunged her long thin hand under the covers, and brought forth a second chick. . . .

The neighbours all wanted to see it. It was passed round from hand to hand, and carefully examined like a phenomenon.

For twenty minutes there were no more births;—then four chicks got out of their shells simultaneously.

And there was a great hum through the assembly. And 'Toine smiled, delighted with his success,—beginning to feel quite proud of this queer paternity. You might say what you please, you never saw many men like him! He was a queer case,—wasn't he?

He observed:

"That makes six. *Nom de nom!*—what a christening!"

And a great burst of laughter went up. A number of strangers entered the tavern. Others were still waiting outside for their chance. People asked each other:

"How many's he got?"

"Got six."

Mother 'Toine carried this new family to the yellow hen;

and the hen clucked crazily, bristled up her feathers, and opened her wings as wide as she could to shelter the ever-increasing multitude of her little ones.

"There's another!" yelled 'Toine.

He was mistaken,—there were three more! It was a triumph! The last chick burst open its shell at 7 o'clock that evening. All the eggs were hatched. And 'Toine, wild with joy, free again, glorious, kissed the little creature on the back,—nearly smothered it with his lips. He wanted to keep that one in his bed—just that one—until next day, feeling seized with a natural affection for the tiny thing to which he had given life; but the old woman took it away like the others in spite of his supplications.

All those present were delighted, and as they went home they talked of nothing else. Horslaville, the last to linger, asked:

"Say, Pap 'Toine,—going to invite me to fricassee the first, eh?"

The face of 'Toine grew radiant at the idea of a fricassee; and the fat man answered:

"For sure, I'll invite you,—for sure, my son-in-law."

HAPPINESS

HAPPINESS

IT was tea-time;—they had not yet brought in the lamps.
The city overlooked the sea; the vanished sun had left the
sky all rosy with his passing, and as if rubbed with dust-
of-gold; and the Mediterranean, without one wrinkle, without one quiver,—smooth and shining under the dying light,—
seemed an immeasurable sheet of polished metal.

Far away to the right the denticulated mountains outlined
their dark profile against the paling purple of the sunset. . . .

They were talking about love,—discussing the old, old subject,—telling things that had been told and retold a thousand
times before. The sweet melancholy of the twilight lent a
languor to their words,—filled their hearts with a vague emotion; and the old word, "love," incessantly repeated, sometimes by the deep voice of a man, sometimes in the lighter
timbre of a woman's speech,—seemed to fill all the little
room,—to flit through it like a bird,—to haunt it like a
ghost

Was it possible to love on for several years.

"Yes," answered some.

"No," declared others.

Then distinctions were made, and demarcations were established, and examples were quoted; and all, men and women,—

moved by suddenly awakened and touching souvenirs, which were ever rising to their lips, but which they could not utter, —seemed full of excitement, and talked, with a deep emotion and an ardent interest, of that commonplace but all-ruling thing: the tender and mysterious accord of two human beings.

But all at once, somebody, looking far away, cried out:

"Oh!—look over there!—what is that?"

From out the sea, at the very verge of the horizon, towered up a grey shape,—enormous and dim.

All the women had risen up, and were looking, without understanding it, at that extraordinary thing they had never seen before.

Someone said:

"That is Corsica! You can see it like that just about two or three times a year,—in certain exceptional conditions of the atmosphere, when the air is perfectly limpid and does not contain those vapory mists which veil distances."

The mountain crests could be confusedly discerned;—some thought they could even distinguish the snow upon the summits, and everybody felt surprised, affected, almost frightened by that sudden apparition of a world,—by that phantom which had risen from the sea. Perhaps visions like these had been seen by those men who, like Columbus, first sailed away into the unknown seas.

Then an old gentleman, who had not said a word the whole evening, observed:

"Listen! I used to know in that very island you now perceive before you,—which seems to have risen into sight in order to answer our questions itself, and has called up to me a very singular reminiscence,—I used to know in that very island one remarkable example of constant love,—of unspeakably happy love.

"Let me tell it to you":

Five years ago I made a trip to Corsica. That wild island is more unknown and, after a fashion, further away from us than America, although it may be seen from the French coast sometimes as it is seen to-day.

Imagine a world still chaotic,—a tempest of mountains separated by narrow ravines where torrents roll,—never a plain, but enormous billows of granite, giant undulations of earth covered with thicket-growths or with lofty forests of chestnut and pine. It is a virgin soil,—uncultivated, desolate,—although you sometimes see a village looking like a heap of loose rocks at the summit of a hill. No agriculture, no industry, no art. You never find such a thing as a piece of carved wood, a bit of cut stone—the least souvenir of ancestral taste, either *naif* or refined, for the graceful or the beautiful. Indeed this is the very fact which most impresses one in that superb and rugged country: the hereditary indifference for that research after attractive form, which we call art.

Italy—where every palace, full of masterpieces, is a masterpiece itself,—where marble, wood, bronze, iron, all metals and all stones attest the genius of man,—where the smallest antique objects lying about the old houses reveal the divine seeking after grace—Italy is for us all the holy fatherland which we love because it shows and proves to us the effort, the grandeur, the power, and the triumph of creative intelligence.

And face to face with her stands Corsica,—just as in the earliest ages of the world. The man lives there in his clumsy dwelling,—careless of everything which bears no relation to his existence or to his family quarrels. And he has retained all the defects and all the merits of uncivilized races,—violent, vindictive, sanguinary without compunction; but also hospitable, generous, devoted, simple, opening his door to every passer-by, and tendering his loyal friendship in exchange for the least mark of sympathy.

. . . Well, I had been wandering over the magnificent island for about a month,—with the sensation of finding myself at the very end of the world. No taverns, no public-houses, no roads. One has to follow the mule-paths in order to reach those little villages which cling to the flanks of the mountains, which overlook tortuous abysses whence you hear of evenings, continually rising, the dull deep roar of torrents. You knock at the door of a house,—you ask shelter for the night, and food enough to last you until morning. Then you can sit at the rude table, and sleep under the humble roof; and in the morning you can press the extended hand of your host, who is sure to accompany you as far as the limits of the village.

Now, one evening, after ten hours' walking, I came to a little dwelling that stood all alone at the further end of a narrow valley, which sloped down to the sea a league away. The two steep sides of the mountain, covered with brush, loose rocks and immense trees, shut in this woefully dismal valley like two dark walls.

Around the hut a few vines were growing, there was a little garden, and some distance off were a few large chestnut trees— just enough to live upon, in short, but a fortune in that poverty-stricken country.

The woman who received me was old, austere and exceptionally neat. The man, seated upon a straw chair, rose to salute me, then sat down again, without a word. His companion said to me:

"You must excuse him; he is deaf now. He is eighty-two years old."

She spoke the French of France. I was surprised.

I asked her:

"You are not a Corsican?"

She replied:

"No; we are from the Continent. But then we have been living here for fifty years."

A sensation of fear and pain came over me at the mere thought of the fifty years spent in that darksome nook—so remote from the cities of men. An aged shepherd came in; and all sat down to the single dish which constituted the dinner of the poor folks—a thick soup of potatoes, lard and cabbages.

When the brief repast was over, I went to sit at the door,

feeling depressed by the melancholy of the gloomy landscape,—and perhaps also by that strange sense of distress
which sometimes seizes travellers on certain dismal evenings,
in certain desolate places, I felt as if everything was about to
end,—life and the universe itself. In such moments one has
a sudden revelation of the hollowness of life, the isolation of
everybody, the nothingness of everything,—the black solitude of the heart that rocks itself to sleep and ever deceives
itself with dreams that are only broken by death.

The old woman soon joined me; and, tortured by that
curiosity which almost smoulders somewhere in the most patient mind, asked me:

"So you are from France?"

"Yes, I am just on a pleasure-trip."

"Perhaps you are from Paris."

"No, I am from Nancy."

It seemed to me that an extraordinary emotion passed
over her. How I saw it, or, rather, felt it, I do not know.

She repeated very slowly:

"So you are from Nancy?"

The man appeared at the door, with his face impassive
as the faces of deaf men are.

She observed:

"It makes no difference; he cannot hear."

After a few seconds she spoke again:

"You know a great many people at Nancy?"

"Why yes,—nearly everybody."

"The Saint-Allaize family?"

"Yes, very well indeed. They were intimate friends of my father."

"What is your name?"

I told her my name. She looked at me fixedly, and then said in that low voice which always accompanies recollection:

"Yes, yes, I remember perfectly well. . . . And the Brismares, what has become of them?"

"They are all dead."

"Ah! And the Sirmonts—do you know them?"

"Yes;—the last one is now a general."

Then, all quivering with emotion,—with anguish,—with I know not what vague, powerful, and sacred feelings,—with I know not what desire to speak, to tell everything, to avow all that she had hitherto hidden away in the very bottom of her heart,—to talk of those whose mere name had so agitated her, she said:

"Yes, Henri de Sirmont. I know him well. He is my brother."

And I raised my eyes to her face, startled with astonishment. And all suddenly an old memory came back to me.

Long years ago, it had made a great scandal in Lorraine. A young girl, beautiful and wealthy, Suzanne de Sirmont, had eloped with a non-commissioned officer of the very same regiment of huzzars that her father commanded.

He was a handsome young man—a son of peasants, indeed,—but looking superb in the blue dolman: this soldier who had made love to the daughter of his colonel. Doubtless she had remarked him first, learned to love him, as she watched the brilliant squadrons wheeling by. But how he had ever managed to speak to her,—how they had ever been able to meet, to come to an understanding,—how she had ever dared to let him know that she loved him,—nobody was ever able to find out.

Nothing had ever been suspected, or feared. One evening, just at the time the soldier's term of service was over, he disappeared with her. They were long looked for, never found. No news was ever obtained concerning them; and all considered her as dead.

And I had found her again in that ghastly valley!

Then I exclaimed, in my turn:

"Yes, I remember it all now. You are Mademoiselle Suzanne."

She nodded her head. Tears were falling from her eyes. Then, with a look directing my attention to the old man at the door, she said:

"That is he."

And I understood that she loved him still,—that she saw him still as when the first sight of him had charmed her girlish eyes.

I asked:

"Tell me, have you been happy?"

She answered in a voice that came right from the heart:

"Oh yes!—very happy. He has always made me very happy. I have never had cause to regret anything."

I looked at her,—made sad, surprised, amazed by the power of love! That rich girl had followed that man—that peasant. She had become a peasant herself. She had accustomed herself to his life—a life without pleasures, without luxuries, without refinements of any kind; she had bowed to all his simple ways. And she loved him still. She had become a country-wife,—wearing the coarse bonnet, the canvas apron. She ate from an earthen plate upon a wooden table—ate cabbage soup, boiled with potatoes and lard. She slept at his side upon a bed of straw.

She had never thought of anything but him! She had never regretted the dainty dresses, or the rich textures, or the elegancies, or the softness of sofas, or the perfumed warmth of curtained rooms, or the caress of downy beds into which delicate bodies plunge for sleep. She had never wanted anything but him;—he was there—she desired nothing more.

She had abandoned life, quite young—and society,—and those who had reared her tenderly, loved her fondly. She had come, alone with him, to dwell in that savage ravine. And he had been everything to her, everything she could wish, everything she had dreamed, everything she had waited for, everything she had hoped for. He had filled her whole existence with happiness, from first to last.

She could not possibly have been more happy.

And all night long, as I listened to the hoarse breathing

of the old soldier lying on his pallet beside her who had followed him from so far away, I kept thinking of that strange and simple adventure, composed of so few incidents.

And I left at sunrise, after shaking hands with the old married pair.

*   *   *   *   *   *   *

The narrator paused. A woman said:

"That is all very well. But she had too facile an ideal,— wants too primitive and exigencies too simple. She must have been silly."

Another woman murmured slowly:

"What matter!—she was happy."

And far away, in the depth of the horizon, Corsica buried herself in the night,—slowly melted back into the sea,—effaced her vast shadow which she seemed to have made visible only in order to tell us the story of those two humble lovers who found shelter on her shores.

HE!

HE!

. . . You ask me why I am going to marry?

I can scarcely dare to confess to you the strange and inconceivable reason which urges me to this insane course.

I am going to marry in order not to be alone.

I do not know how to tell it,—how to make myself understood. You will pity me and you will despise me when you know in what a wretched state of mind I am.

I do not want to be alone any more,—at night. I want to feel some being near me, close to me,—a being that can speak, say something, no matter what.

I want to be able to rouse that being from sleep—to be able to ask that being any question suddenly,—even a stupid question, so that I can feel my dwelling is inhabited,—so that I can know that a mind is awake, that a reasoning-power is at work,—so that, if I suddenly light my candle I can see a human face beside me . . . because . . . because . . . (how can I dare avow my shame!) . . . because I am afraid when I am by myself.

Oh! you do not yet comprehend me!

I am not afraid of any danger. If a man were to come in, I would kill him without a shudder. I have no fear of ghosts;—I do not believe in the supernatural. I am not afraid of the dead;—I believe in the total annihilation of every human being that passes away!

Then! . . . yes. Then! . . . well! I am afraid of myself! I am afraid of being afraid,—afraid of the mental spasms that are driving me mad,—afraid of the horrible sense of incomprehensible terror.

Laugh if you please! It is hideous; it is incurable. I am afraid of the walls, of the furniture, of familiar objects which seem to me to become animated with a sort of animal life. Above all I am afraid of the horrible confusion of my mind, the confusion of my reason which goes from me, all befogged, dissipated by some mysterious and inexplicable anguish.

First, I feel a vague disquiet that passes into my mind, and makes all my flesh creep. I look around me. Nothing! And I feel a need of something. Of what? Something incomprehensible. Then I become afraid, simply because I cannot comprehend my own fear.

I speak!—I am frightened by my own voice. I walk!— then I am frightened by the Unknown which is behind the door, or behind the curtain, or inside the armoir, or under the bed. And nevertheless I know perfectly well there is really nothing in any of those places.

I turn round suddenly because I am afraid of what is behind me,—although there is really nothing behind me, and although I know it!

I become nervous; I feel the scare growing upon me; and I lock myself into my room, and I bury myself in my bed, and I hide myself under my bedclothes; and, cowering there, gathering myself up like a ball, I shut my eyes in desperation, and thus remain for a seemingly infinite length of time, oppressed by the thought that my candle is still burning on the little table beside the bed, and that I should really blow it out. And I dare not!

Is it not frightful to be in such a condition?

There was a time when I never felt this way. I used to go home feeling perfectly calm. I went out and came in without anything to trouble the serenity of my mind. If I had then been told what a stupid and terrible disease of fear,—of incredible fear, would come upon me in after days, I would certainly have laughed! I used to open the doors in the dark with perfect confidence; I used to make my preparations for going to bed, quietly, without even bolting myself in; and I never thought of getting up in the middle of the night to see if all the entrances to my room were strongly secured.

The trouble began last year in a singular way.

It was in autumn,—on a certain damp evening. When my housekeeper had taken her departure, after I had dined, I asked myself what I was going to do. For some time I walked up and down my room. I felt myself weary, unreasonably depressed, incapable of doing any work,—lacking even the mental force to read. A fine rain was moistening the windowpanes; I was melancholy—all permeated by one of those causeless attacks of despondency which make you feel inclined to cry,—which make a man want to talk to somebody or anybody in order to shake off the weight of one's own fancies.

I felt lonesome. Never before did my dwelling seem to me so empty. An infinite and heart-sickening solitude surrounded me. What was I to do? I sat down. Then a nervous impatience seemed to pass into my legs. I got up and began to walk again. Perhaps I was also a little feverish; for my hands,—clasped behind my back as one's hands often are when one walks about leisurely,—seemed to burn one another where they touched, and I noticed it. Then a sudden cold shudder ran down my back. I thought that the outside dampness was entering the room; and the idea occurred to me that it would be well to light a fire. I lit it; it was the first of the year. And I sat down once more, watching the flame. But soon the impossibility of remaining quiet in any one position forced me to get up again; and I felt that I would have to go out somewhere, to stir myself, to find a friend.

I went out. First I visited the houses of three different friends—no one of whom was at home; then I went on the boulevard, resolved to find some acquaintance or other.

It was dismal everywhere. The wet sidewalks were shining. A waterly lukewarmness,—one of those lukewarmnesses which nevertheless chill you with sudden shivers,—the weighty lukewarmness of impalpable rain,—seemed to bear down over the whole street, and to make the gas-jets burn wearily and dim.

I walked along sluggishly, saying over and over again to myself: "I won't find anybody to talk to."

Several times I looked into all the *cafés* between La Madeleine and the Faubourg Poissonniere. Only miserable-looking people, who did not seem to have even vim enough to finish what they had ordered, were sitting at the tables.

I wandered about in this way for a long time; and about midnight I took my way home. I was quite calm, but very tired. My concierge, who always goes to bed before eleven o'clock, opened the door for me at once, contrary to his usual habit; and I thought to myself: "Hello! some other lodger must have just gone upstairs."

Whenever I go out I always double-lock my door. This time I found it simply pulled-to; and the fact impressed me. I thought that perhaps some letters might have been brought upstairs during the evening.

I went in. My fire was still burning, even brightly enough to light up the apartment. I took the candle in order to kindle it at the grate, when, as I looked right before me, I saw some one sitting in my easy chair, with his back turned to me,—apparently warming his feet at the fire.

I was not startled at all—no! not the least in the world! A very natural supposition occurred to me,—namely, that one of my friends had come to pay me a visit. The concierge, to whom I had given instructions when I went out, had naturally told the visitor that I would soon be back, and had lent his own key. And then all the other incidents of my return flashed through my mind in a second,—the opening of the door at once,—my own door simply pulled-to, etc.

My friend,—whose hair alone I could see over the back of the chair,—had evidently dropped asleep while waiting for my return; and I proceeded to wake him up. I then got a distinct view of him;—his right arm hung down; his feet were crossed one over the other; and the way his head drooped, a little to the left of the arm-chair, showed plainly enough that he was asleep. I asked myself: "Who is it?" Anyhow the light in the room was not strong enough to see perfectly by. I put out my hand to touch his shoulder! . . .

My hand touched only the wood of the chair! Nobody was there! The chair was empty!

Mercy! What a shock it gave me!

First I leaped back as if some terrible peril had made itself visible.

Then I turned round, feeling that somebody was behind me;—then, almost as quickly, an imperative desire to look at that chair again, made me wheel round a second time. And I stood there, panting with fear,—so bewildered as to be incapable of thinking,—on the very point of falling.

But I am by nature a cool man; and my self-possession soon returned. I thought to myself: "I have just had a hallucination—that is all!" And I immediately began to reflect on the phenomenon. In such moments the mind operates very rapidly.

I had had an hallucination—that was an incontestable fact. Now my mind had all the time remained clear,—performing its functions regularly and logically. There was consequently no real affection of the brain. The eyes alone had been deluded and had deluded my imagination. The eyes had a vision—one of those visions that make simple-minded folks believe in miracles. It was simply a nervous accident to the optical apparatus—nothing more;—perhaps there was a slight congestion.

And I lighted my candle. As I bent down over the fire I found myself trembling; and I drew myself up again with a sudden start, as if some one had touched me from behind.

Certainly my nerves were out of order.

I walked to and fro for a little while; I talked aloud to myself. I hummed a few airs.

Then I double-locked the door of my room; and I began to feel somewhat reassured. At all events nobody could get in.

Again I sat down; and for a long time I thought over my adventure. Then I went to bed, and blew out my light.

For a few minutes everything seemed all right. I remained lying quietly on my back. Then I felt an irresistible desire to take a look at my room; and I turned over on my side.

My fire held only two or three red embers, which barely lighted the legs of the chair; and I thought I saw the Man sitting there again.

I struck a match quickly. But I had been mistaken; I could see nothing!

Nevertheless I got up, took the chair, and placed it out of sight behind my bed.

Then I made everything dark again, and tried to go to

sleep. I could not have sunk into unconsciousness for more than five minutes, when I saw in a dream, and as distinctly as reality itself, the whole incident of that evening. I woke up in terror, and after making a light, sat up in bed without daring to try to go to sleep again.

Sleep, notwithstanding, twice seized upon me for a few moments, in spite of myself. Twice I saw the same thing. I thought I had actually gone mad!

When daylight appeared I felt completely cured, and I took a peaceful sleep until midday.

It had passed,—entirely passed. I had had a fever, a nightmare, or something of that sort. Anyhow I had been sick. Nevertheless I thought myself very much of a fool.

That day I was quite jolly. I dined at the *cabaret,* went to the theatre, and then started for home. But lo! as I drew near my house, a strange sense of uneasiness took possession of me. I was afraid of seeing him again,—*Him!* Not afraid of Him precisely,—not afraid of his presence, in which I did not believe; but afraid of another optical trouble, afraid of the hallucination, afraid of the fear which would come upon me.

For more than an hour I kept walking up and down the sidewalk;—then at last I decided this was absolute folly, and I went in. I panted so much that I could scarcely climb the stairs. I stood for fully ten minutes more on the landing, in front of my room;—then, suddenly, I felt a rush of courage, a bracing up of will. I plunged my key in the key-

hole,—I rushed forward with a lighted candle in my hand,—
I kicked in the unfastened door of the room,—and I threw
one terrified glance at the fireplace. I saw nothing,—Ah! . . .

What a relief! What joy! What a deliverance! I went to
and fro with a swaggering air. But still I did not feel perfectly confident;—I would turn round by fits and starts to
look behind me; the darkness in the corners of the room
frightened me.

I slept badly—being incessantly startled out of my rest
by imaginary noises. But I never saw Him. No. That was
all over.

Ever since that day I have been afraid to be alone at night.
I can *feel* it there, close to me—the Vision! It did not make
its appearance again—oh, no! And what matter, anyhow,
since I don't believe in it,—since I know that it is nothing?

Still it annoys me, because I keep all the time thinking
about it. . . . One arm was hanging down on the right side;
his head drooped a little to the left, like that of a man
asleep. . . . Come, that's enough of it, *nom de Dieu!* I don't
want to think about it any more!

And still, what is this feeling of being haunted? Why does
it persist in this way? . . . His feet were quite close to the fire.

He haunts me;—it is madness, but it is so! Who is He?
I know perfectly well that He does not exist,—that it is nothing whatever! He only exists in my apprehension, in my fear,
in my anguish! . . . There!—that's enough! . . .

Yes, but it is no use for me to reason with myself about it;—no use to try to brace up against it;—I can't remain alone at home any more, because He is there! I know I won't see him any more;—he won't show himself again—that's past. But he is there all the same, in my thought. Because he remains invisible, it does not follow that he is not there! He is behind the doors, and in the armoir and under the bed—in all the dark corners, in all the shadows. If I stir the door upon its hinges,—if I open my armoir,—if I lower my light to look under the bed,—if I throw the light upon the corners, upon the shadows,—he is not there; but then I feel him behind me! I turn round—certain all the while that I am not going to see him, that I will not ever see him again. He is behind me still, for all that!

It is stupid,—but it is atrocious! What would you have me do? I can do nothing!

But if there were two of us together at home, then, I feel—yes I am perfectly sure—that he would not be there any more. For he is there because I am alone,—and for no other reason than because I am alone.

THE DOWRY

THE DOWRY

NOBODY was surprised by the marriage of Maître Simon Lebrument and Mademoiselle Jeanne Cordier. Maître Lebrument had just purchased the notary-practice of Maître Papillon:—of course a good deal of money had to be paid for it; and Mademoiselle Jeanne had three hundred thousand francs ready cash,—in bank notes and money at call.

Maître Lebrument was a handsome young man, who had style,—a notarial style, a provincial style,—but anyhow style, and style was a rare thing at Boutigny-le-Rebours.

Mademoiselle Cordier had natural grace and a fresh complexion;—her grace may have been a little marred by awkwardness of manner, and her complexion was not set off to advantage by her style of dressing; but for all that she was a fine girl, well worth wooing and winning.

The wedding turned all Boutigny topsy-turvy.

The married pair, who found themselves the subject of much admiration, returned to the conjugal domicile to hide their happiness,—having resolved to make only a little trip to Paris after first passing a few days together at home. . . .

At the end of four days, Madame Lebrument simply worshipped her husband. She could not exist a single moment without him; she had to have him all day near her to pet him, to kiss him, to play with his hands, his beard, his nose, etc. Sitting upon his lap, she would take him by both ears and say: "Open your mouth and shut your eyes!" Then he would open his lips with confidence, half close his eyes, and receive a very tender and very long kiss, that would make a sort of electrical shiver run down his back. And he, for his part, did not have caresses enough, lips enough, hands enough— did not have enough of himself in short, to adore his wife with from morning till evening and from evening until morning.

*   *   *   *   *   *   *

After the first week passed, he said to his young companion:

"If you like, we'll start for Paris next Tuesday. We'll do like lovers before they get married:—we'll go to the restaurants, the theatres, the concert halls, everywhere, everywhere."

She jumped for joy.

"Oh! yes,—oh! yes; let us go just as soon as possible!"

He continued:

"And then, as we must not forget anything, tell your father in advance to have your dowry all ready;—I will take it with us, and while I have the chance to see Maître Papillon, I might as well pay him."

"I'll tell him first thing to-morrow morning."

And then he seized her in his arms to recommence that little petting game which she had learned to love so much during the previous eight days.

The following Tuesday the father-in-law and mother-in-law

went to the railroad depot with their daughter and their son-in-law, who were off for Paris.

The step-father said:

"I swear to you it is not prudent to carry so much money in your pocketbook."

The young notary smiled:

"Don't worry yourself at all, *beau-papa;*—I'm used to these things. You must understand that in this profession of mine it sometimes happens that I have nearly a million on my person. As it is, we can escape going through a heap of formalities and delays. Don't worry yourself about us."

An employé shouted:

"All aboard for Paris!"

They rushed into a car where two old ladies were already, installed.

Lebrument whispered in his wife's ear:

"This is annoying;—I shan't be able to smoke."

She answered in an undertone:

"Yes, it annoys me too,—but not on account of your cigar."

The engine whistled, and the train started. The trip lasted a full hour, during which they said little or nothing to each other, because the two old women would not go to sleep.

As soon as they found themselves in the Saint-Lazare station, Maître Lebrument said to his wife:

"If you like, darling, we'll first breakfast somewhere on the boulevard,—then we'll come back leisurely for our baggage and have it taken to the hotel."

She consented at once.

"Oh! yes—let us breakfast at the restaurant. Is it far?"

He answered:

"Yes, it's rather far; but we'll take the omnibus."

She was surprised

"Why not take a hack?"

He scolded her smilingly:

"And that is your idea of economy, eh? A hack for five minutes' ride at the rate of six sous a minute! You could not deny yourself anything,—eh?"

"You are right," she murmured, feeling a little confused.

A big omnibus, drawn by three horses, came along at full trot.

Lebrument shouted:

"Driver!—hey, driver!"

The ponderous vehicle paused. And the young notary, pushing his wife before him, said to her in a very quick tone:

"Get inside! I'm going on top to smoke a cigarette before breakfast."

She did not have time to answer. The conductor, who had already caught her by the arm in order to help her up the step, almost pitched her into the vehicle; and she fell bewildered upon a bench, looking through the rear window, with stupefaction, at the feet of her husband ascending to the top of the conveyance.

And she sat there motionless between a big fat man who stunk of tobacco, and an old woman who smelled of dog.

All the other passengers, sitting dumbly in line—(a grocery boy; a working woman;—an infantry sergeant;—a gold-spectacled gentleman, wearing a silk hat with an enormous brim, turned up at each side like a gutter-pipe;—two ladies with a great air of self-importance and a snappy manner, whose very look seemed to say, "We are here; but we do not put ourselves on any level with this crowd!"—two good Sisters;— a girl with long hair; and an undertaker)—all had the look of a lot of caricatures, a museum of grotesques, a series of ludicrous cartoons of the human face—like those rows of absurd puppets at fairs, which people knock down with balls.

The jolts of the vehicle made all their heads sway, shook them, made the flaccid skin of their cheeks shake; and as the noise of the wheels gradually stupefied them, they seemed so many sleeping idiots.

The young wife remained there, inert:

"Why did he not come in with me?" she kept asking herself.

A vague sadness oppressed her. Surely he might very well have afforded to deny himself that one cigarette!

The two good Sisters signed to the driver to stop, and got out, one after the other. The omnibus went on, and stopped again. And a cook came in, all red-faced and out of breath. She sat down, and put her market basket on her knees. A strong odour of dishwater filled the omnibus.

"Why, it is much further away than I thought," said Jeanne to herself.

The undertaker got out, and was succeeded by a coachman

who smelled of stables. The long-haired girl had for successor a messenger whose feet exhaled an odor of perspiration.

The notary's wife felt ill-at-ease, sick, ready to cry without knowing why.

Other persons got out; others got in. The omnibus still rolled on through interminable streets, stopping at stations, and proceeding again on its way.

"How far it is!" said Jeanne to herself. "Suppose that he forgot, or went to sleep! He was very tired anyhow. . . ."

Gradually all the passengers got out. She alone remained. The driver cried out:

"Vaugirard!"

As she did not stir, he called again:

"Vaugirard!"

She stared at him, vaguely comprehending that he must be addressing her, since there was no one else in the omnibus. For the third time the driver yelled:

"Vaugirard!"

She asked him:

"Where are we?"

He answered in a tone of irritation:

"We're at Vaugirard, *parbleu!*—that's the twentieth time I've been hollering it!"

"Is it far from the boulevard?" she asked.

"What boulevard?"

"The Boulevard des Italienes."

"We passed that ages ago!"

"Ah! . . . Please be so kind as to let my husband know."

"Your husband?—Where's he?"

"Up on top——"

"Up on top! There hasn't been anyone outside for ever so long!"

She threw up her hands in terror:

"How is that? It can't be possible! He came with me, on the omnibus. Look again, please!—he must be there!"

The driver became rude:

"Here, here! that's enough talk for you, little one. One man lost,—ten to be found. Scoot now!—the trip's over. You'll find another man in the street if you want one."

Tears came to her eyes:—she persisted:

"Oh, sir, you are mistaken,—I assure you, you are mistaken. He had a great big pocketbook under his arm. . . ."

The employé began to laugh:

"A great big pocketbook. Ah! yes—he got down at La Madeleine. It's all the same,—he's dropped you pretty smartly—ha! ha! ha! . . ."

The vehicle had stopped. She got out, and in spite of herself glanced up instinctively at the roof of the omnibus. It was absolutely deserted.

* * * * * * *

Then she began to cry out loud, without thinking that everybody would hear her and see her. She sobbed:

"What is going to become of me?"

The superintendent of the station approached, and demanded:

"What is the matter?"

The driver responded in a mischievous tone:

"It's a lady whose husband gave her the slip on the trip."

The other replied:

"Well, that is nothing to you—you just mind your own business!"

And he turned on his heel.

Then she began to walk straight ahead,—too much bewildered and terrified to even comprehend what had happened to her. Where was she to go? What was she to do? What on earth could have happened to him? How could he have made such a mistake?—how could he have so ill-treated her?—how could he have so forgotten himself?—how could he have been so absent-minded?

She had just two francs in her pocket. Who could she go to? All of a sudden she thought of her cousin Barral, assistant superintendent in the naval department office.

She had just enough to pay for a hack; and she had herself driven to his residence. And she met him just as he was leaving the house to go to the office. He had just such another big pocketbook under his arm as Lebrument had.

She jumped from the hack.

"Henry!" she cried.

He stopped in astonishment.

"What! Jeanne!—you here? all alone? . . . why what is the matter?—where have you come from?"

She stammered out, with her eyes full of tears:

"I lost my husband a little while ago."

"Lost him—where?"

"On an omnibus."

"On an omnibus? . . . Oh!"

Then she told him all her adventure, with tears.

He listened thoughtfully. He asked:

"Well, was his head perfectly clear this morning?"

"Yes."

"Good! Did he have much money about him?"

"Yes,—he had my dowry——"

"Your dowry?—the whole of it?"

"Yes, the whole of it . . . to pay for his practice."

"Well! well! my dear cousin, your husband must at this very moment be making tracks for Belgium."

Still she did not understand. She stammered:

"You say my husband . . . is, you say? . . ."

"I say that he has swindled you out of your—your capital . . . that's all there is about it!"

She stood there panting, suffocating;—she murmured:

"Then he is . . . he is . . . he is a scoundrel!"

And completely overcome by emotion, she hid her face against her cousin's vest, sobbing.

As people were stopping to look at them, he pushed her

very gently inside the house, and guided her up the stairs, with his arm about her waist. And, as his astonished housekeeper opened the door, he said:

"Sophie, go to the restaurant at once, and order breakfast for two. I shall not go to the office to-day."

A WALK

A WALK

When old Leras, the bookkeeper of Messrs. Labuze & Co., left the warehouse, he remained dazzled for a moment by the sunlight. He had been working all day under the yellow light of the gas-jets in the back office, which looked out upon a court as narrow and deep as a well. The little room in which he had thus passed his days for forty long years, even in the hottest part of summer, was so gloomy that it was very seldom possible to avoid keeping the gas burning from 11 a. m. to 3 p. m.

It was always damp and cold there; and the emanations of the grave-like court upon which the window opened, entered into the darksome room, filling it with an odour of mould and a stench of gutters.

Regularly for forty long years, M. Leras had come to this dungeon at eight o'clock in the morning, to remain there until seven in the evening, stooping over his books, continually writing with the systematic application of a good employé.

He now earned a salary of 3000 francs a year,—having begun at only 1500 francs. He had remained a bachelor, because his means had never permitted him to marry. And as he had never had any pleasures, he had very little to wish for. Nevertheless from time to time, when weary of his monotonous and never-ending task, he would express the platonic desire:—

"Christi!—if I only had a revenue of 5000 francs, wouldn't I take things easy!"

The fact was he had never been able to "take things easy" —as he had never had anything more than his regular monthly salary.

His life had passed without any noteworthy incidents, without any emotions, and almost without any hopes. The faculty of dreaming, which every human being has within him, had never been developed in the mediocrity of his ambitions.

He had entered the employ of Messrs. Labuze & Co. when he was twenty-one years of age; and he had never left them.

He had lost his father in 1856—and then his mother, in 1859. And since that time nothing remarkable had happened to him, except that in 1868 he had been obliged to move his lodgings because his landlord wished to raise the rent.

Every morning his alarm-clock made him jump out of bed at 6 o'clock precisely,—by a frightful noise like a coil of chain suddenly unrolled.

Twice—in 1866 and in 1874—the alarm-clock had got out of order, without his having ever been able to find out the reason why. He used, after dressing himself, to make his own bed, sweep out his own room, dust his chair and the top of his bureau. All these little jobs occupied about an hour and a half of his time.

Then he would go out, buy a loaf at the Lahure bakery, which had changed proprietors without changing its name eleven different times since he began to go there; and he would wend his way to the office, nibbling the bread as he walked along.

His whole life had been thus passed in the one narrow office, whose walls had always been papered with the same wall-paper. He had entered it young, as the assistant of M. Brument, whose position he had some day hoped to fill.

He filled it now; and had nothing more to hope for.

All that harvest of souvenirs which other men gather in the course of their lives,—exciting incidents, sweet or tragical amours, adventurous travels, all the hazards of a free life had remained unknown to him.

The days, the weeks, the months, the seasons, the years, had succeeded each other in exactly the same way. At the same hours each day he got up, went out, entered the office, breakfasted, left, dined, and retired to bed; nothing had ever interrupted the monotony of the same acts, the same facts, and the same thoughts.

Once he used to see his own blonde moustache and curly fair hair in the little round looking-glass left by his predecessor. Now he was wont to contemplate in the same glass, each evening, before going home, his white moustache and his bald forehead. Forty years had rolled by,—tedious, yet swift, all empty as a day of mourning, and each one as like the other as the hours of a restless night! Forty years of which nothing remained,—not even a memory, not even a misfortune, since the death of his parents. Nothing.

*　　　*　　　*　　　*　　　*　　　*　　　*

This day, M. Leras remained standing at the street door, dazzled by the splendour of the setting sun; and instead of returning at once home, he thought he would take a little walk before dinner,—an idea which only occurred to him about four or five times a year.

He reached the boulevards, where the great torrent of life was flowing by, under the budding trees. It was a spring evening;—one of those first languid, warm evenings which fill hearts with the intoxication of life.

M. Leras walked with the sprightly step of a hale old man: he had a merriment in his eyes—he felt joyful with the universal joy and the tepid warmth of the evening air.

He reached the Champs-Elysées, and still continued on,— feeling reanimated by the breath of rejuvenescent life which seemed to come with every breeze.

The whole sky flamed;—and the Arc de Triomphe outlined its black mass against the blazing background of the horizon, like a giant standing in the midst of a conflagration. When he reached the vicinity of the monstrous monument, the old bookkeeper felt hungry, and he went to a wine-room to get his dinner.

They served him with a *pied de mouton-poulette,* a salad, and some asparagus, at a little table in front of the establishment, upon the sidewalk; and M. Leras enjoyed the best dinner he had had for many a day. He washed down his bit of Brie cheese with a half-bottle of first class Bordeaux; then he took a cup of black coffee,—which was a thing he seldom indulged in,—and finally a very small glass of fine champagne.

After paying his bill, he felt quite lively, quite jolly, even a little too much so. And he said to himself: "What a lovely evening! I believe I'll walk on as far as the entrance to the Bois de Boulogne. It will do me good."

He went on. An old, old air, that he had heard a girl-neighbour singing many years ago, would keep obstinately running through his head:

> Quand le bois reverdit,
> Mon amoureux me dit:
> Viens respirer, ma belle,
> Sous la tonnelle.

He hummed it unceasingly,—began it over and over again. Night had descended upon Paris,—a windless and fervid night. M. Leras followed the Avenue du Bois de Boulogne, and looked at the carriages passing. They kept coming, with their big shining eyes, one after the other—each allowing a moment's glimpse of some reclining couple within, with arms intertwined about each other: the woman always in some light-coloured robe, the man in black.

It was one long procession of lovers passing under the starry and fervid sky. They kept on coming, always, always,—leaning back in their open carriages, speechless, pressing close to one another,—lost in hallucination, in the emotion of the heart, in the inexpressible anticipation of bliss to come. All the warm gloom seemed full of kisses—flitting, hovering. A sense of tenderness lent languor to the very air,—made it breathless! All those beings intertwined—all those beings intoxicated by the same hope, the same expectation, the same thought, made something like a fever in the atmosphere about them. All those vehicles, full of caresses, seemed to leave in their wake a sort of vertiginous and subtle emanation.

M. Leras, a little tired of walking at last, sat down upon a bench to watch the passage of all those love-burdened carriages. And almost immediately a woman came, and took a seat by his side.

"Good-evening, little man!" she said.

He did not answer. She spoke again. . . .

He said:

"Madame, you do not seem to know who you are addressing."

She slipped her arm under his:

"Now here!—do not be mean,—listen. . . ."

But he had already risen up and walked off,—sick at heart.

A hundred yards further on, another woman accosted him. . . . M. Leras became nervous. Other women passed by him, —calling, inviting him.

It seemed to him that something black had descended upon him,—a sense of desolation.

And he sat down again upon a bench. And still the carriages kept rolling by.

"It would have been better for me not to have come here," he thought;—"now my evening is all spoiled. . . ."

He began to think of all that love, passionate or venal,—of all those kisses, freely given or purchased,—which defiled before him.

Love!—he knew scarcely anything about it. In his whole life he had had but two or three little love incidents,—incidents of chance, unexpected. . . . And he thought also about that life he had lived, so different from the life of others,—so dismal, so sad, so vapid, so empty!

There are indeed human creatures who appear to have no luck in this world. . . . And, all suddenly, as if a thick veil had been rent away from before his eyes, he discerned the misery, the pettiness, the wretched monotony of his existence,— wretchedness past, wretchedness present, wretchedness to come,—the last days to be like the first,—nothing to look forward to, nothing to look back to, nothing around him, nothing even in his heart, nothing anywhere!

And still the long procession of carriages continued to roll by. Incessantly he still saw appear and disappear,—in the rapid passage of each open vehicle,—the two silent figures wrapped in each other's arms. It seemed to him as if all humanity were filing by before him,—drunk with joy, with pleasure, with happiness. And he was there all alone, looking at it,—alone, absolutely alone. He would be alone again to-morrow,—still alone, alone as nobody else in the world was alone.

He rose up, took a few steps, and then, suddenly feeling as fatigued as if he had made a very long journey, sat down again upon the next bench.

What was he waiting for? What was he hoping for? Nothing. He thought it must be nice, when one is old, to find on coming home, little babbling children waiting for you. It is easy to grow old when one is surrounded by those creatures who owe you life, who love you, who caress you, who say to you all those charming little foolish things which warm one's heart and console one for everything else.

And thinking of his empty room,—his miserable little clean room,—into which no one had ever entered except himself, a feeling of distress seemed to strangle his soul. That room seemed to him now even more gloomy than his little office.

No one ever came to it; no one ever spoke in it. It was dead, dumb, without the echo of a human voice. It would seem as if walls sooner or later begin to reflect something of the human nature that lives between them—something of their manner, their features, their ideas. Houses inhabited by happy families have always a more pleasant aspect than the dwellings of miserable people. His room was as void of souvenirs as his life. And the thought of having to re-enter that room, all alone,—to lie down again in that bed,—to begin all over again all the actions and the necessities of every day, terrified him. And as if desiring to fool himself still further away from his ghastly lodging, and further away from the moment of returning to it, he entered a grove of trees to seat himself upon the grass. . . .

He heard all about him, above him, everywhere, a confused, immense, continuous murmur,—a murmur made up of innumerable and varying sounds,—a deep, near and yet far-off murmur,—a vague and enormous palpitation of life: the respiration of Paris, breathing like a colossal being. . . .

*   *   *   *   *   *   *

The sun was already high,—showering down a flood of light upon the Bois du Boulogne. A few carriages commenced to pass;—riders were coming merrily.

A couple were slowly riding along a deserted path. The young woman, suddenly looking up, saw something dark among the branches; she shaded her eyes with her hand—astonished and uneasy.

"Look! . . . what is that?"

Then with a scream she let herself fall into the arms of her companion, who had to lift her from her horse.

The police, being summoned, took down the body of an old man who had hung himself with his suspenders.

It was proven that the death must have occurred the evening before. The papers found on the old man showed that he was a bookkeeper in the employ of Messrs. Labuze & Co., and that his name was Leras.

His death was attributed to suicide—for which no motive could be assigned. Perhaps a momentary fit of insanity!

COCO

COCO

THE farm of the Lucas family was known through all the country round by the name of the *"Métairie."* Nobody could have told why. Doubtless the peasants must have attached to that word "métairie" some idea of wealth and greatness; for the farm was certainly the most vast, the most opulent, and the best managed in all the district.

The immense court,—surrounded by five rows of magnificent trees to protect the thick-set, but delicate, apple trees from the violent winds of the plain,—inclosed a number of long tile-covered buildings for the storage of forage and grain, some handsome cowhouses constructed with walls of silex, stables for thirty horses, and a dwelling-house of red brick, which looked like a small chateau.

The manure-heaps were well-kept; the watchdogs lived in good kennels; a whole nation of chickens ran about in the high grass.

Every day at noon fifteen persons,—masters, valets, and servants,—took their places around the great kitchen-table on which the soup smoked in a huge delf dish, decorated with blue-flower designs.

The animals—horses, cows, pigs and sheep,—were all plump, well cared for, and clean; and Master Lucas himself, a tall man who was beginning to take on flesh, made his regular round three times a day, watching over everything and never forgetting anything.

In the further end of the stable-building, a very old white horse was kept, which the mistress of the establishment wished to support until he should die of old age, because she had raised him, had always kept him, and because he was associated in her memory with many pleasant souvenirs.

A labourer's apprentice, fifteen years old, named Isodor Duval, but more familiarly called Zidore, used to take charge of this invalid, and carry him, all through the winter, his measure of oats and hay. In summer he had to lead him out four times a day to the hill-slope, where he was tethered at such a spot as would afford him all the fresh grass he could eat.

The animal, almost palsied, could only with difficulty move his heavy legs, all bulged out at the knees and swollen above the hoofs. His blanched hide, never curried now, seemed hoary with age, and the very long hairs of his eyelids gave his eyes a sad look.

When Zidore led him out to grass, he had to pull hard at the rope, so slowly did the creature move; and the lad, bending double with his exertions, panted and swore, working himself into a passion at having to take care of such an old hack.

The farm-hands, observing the exasperation of the young fellow against Coco, made plenty of fun for themselves over it. They talked incessantly to Zidore about the horse, just to get him mad. His comrades joked him about it. In the village they nicknamed him Coco-Zidore.

The lad became furious, and felt within him a growing desire to revenge himself upon the horse. He was a lean boy, with long legs,—a boy always dirty, with a shock of red thick, coarse, bristling hair. He had a stupid look, spoke only in stammers with infinite difficulty, as if ideas were striving in vain to form within his dull brutish mind.

As it was he had wondered for a long time why Coco was kept,—feeling angry to see so much good provender wasted upon a useless beast. It seemed to him an injustice to nourish the creature a moment longer than it could work; it seemed to him revolting to waste oats, oats that cost so dear, on the paralyzed old jade. And often in spite of the express orders of Master Lucas, he would economize upon the horse's feed,— giving him only half-measure,—saving on his straw and his hay. And a hatred began to grow up in his vague and childish mind,—the hate such as a rapacious peasant feels,—a sly, ferocious, brutal, and cowardly peasant.

*   *   *   *   *   *   *

When summer came, he had again to go every day several times to *move* the beast from one part of the meadow-slope to another. More and more furious every morning the labourer's boy would start off, with his heavy, trudging step. The men working in the fields would yell at him, as he passed, for a joke:

"Hey! Zidore,—give my compliments to Coco!"

He did not answer a word, but as he walked on he broke off a stout switch from the hedge, and as soon as he had changed the old horse's picket, he let him begin browsing again: then, treacherously going behind him, he lashed his legs. The animal tried to run, to kick, to get away from the blows, and turned in a circle at the end of his rope as if he were inclosed in a track. And the boy flogged him with rage, running behind him, beat him with frenzy, clenching his teeth with fury.

Then he walked off slowly without looking round, while the horse with ribs protruding, completely winded by having run so much, watched him going with his aged eyes. And he did not bend down his bony white head to the grass again until he had seen the blue blouse of the young peasant disappear in the distance.

As the nights were warm, Coco was now allowed to sleep out there, on the edge of the ravine, behind the woods. Zidore alone went to see him.

The boy also amused himself by throwing stones at him. He would sit down, ten steps away from him, upon the declivity, and remain there a whole half-hour,—from time to time flinging a sharp flint at the jade, who remained standing bound before his enemy, and looked at him all the time—not daring to graze until he should be gone.

But this one question always remained fixed in the mind of the labourer's boy: "What is the use of feeding a horse that can't do anything?" It seemed to him that the miserable jade was robbing others of food, was stealing the rightful possessions of man, the gift of God,—was robbing him also, Zidore, who had to work.

Then, little by little every day, the boy began to diminish the breadth of the strip of pasturage he gave the horse, by moving the picket less and less far.

The animal starved, became leaner, wasted away. Too weak to break his tether, he stretched out his neck toward the tall green shining grass, that was so near, and the odor of which rose to his nostrils though he could not reach it.

But one morning an idea came to Zidore: it was simply this,—not to move Coco any more. He had had enough of this trotting so far for the old carcass!

Nevertheless he came, just to enjoy his vengeance. The anxious animal stared at him. He did not beat it that day. He simply walked around it, with his hands in his pockets. He even made as if he was going to move the picket; but he only lifted it, put it down again in the same hole, and walked off, delighted with his discovery.

The horse, seeing him go, whinnied after him to call him back; but the labourer's boy began to run, leaving him all alone in his valley, well-secured, and without one blade of grass in reach of his jaws.

The famished horse tried to reach the rich verdure that he could almost touch with the tip of his nostrils. He went down on his knees, stretched out his neck, protruded his big dribbling lips. It was all in vain. All day the aged animal exhausted himself in useless efforts, in terrible efforts. Hunger was devouring him,—a hunger rendered more frightful by the actual view of all that green nourishment which reached away to the horizon.

The labourer's boy did not come back that day. He wandered about in the woods, looking for nests.

He made his appearance again the following morning. Coco, exhausted, had laid down. He got up on seeing the boy, expecting at last to have his grazing place changed.

But the little peasant did not even so much as look at the mallet that was lying there in the grass. He approached, looked at the horse, flung a lump of clay at his nose that burst all over the white hair, and then went off again, whistling.

The horse remained standing as long as he could see Zidore: then, feeling convinced that all his efforts to reach the neighbouring grass would be useless, he laid down again, and closed his eyes.

Next day Zidore did not come at all.

When, on the day after, he approached the still prostrate Coco, he perceived that he was dead.

Then he stood there, staring at him,—well satisfied with his work,—surprised that it had been finished so soon. He touched him with his foot, lifted one of his legs,—then let it fall again: sat down upon the carcass, and remained there some time, with his eyes fixed upon the grass, thinking about nothing.

He went back to the farm, but told no one of the occurrence; because he wanted another chance to loaf during the time when he had been accustomed to look after the horse.

He went to look at the carcass next day. Crows flew away at his approach. Flies innumerable were hovering and buzzing about the remains.

On going back to the farm he announced the event. The animal was so old that nobody was surprised. The master said to two of his men:

"Take your spades; you can dig a hole there where he is."

And the men buried the horse just on the spot where he had died of hunger.

And the grass soon shot up, stiff green, vigorous,—nourished by the poor body.

THE CHILD

THE CHILD

M. Lemonnier was a widower, with one child. He had loved his wife madly, with a tender and ecstatic love, which had never weakened for so much as a single instant during the whole of their married life. He was a good man, an upright man—simple-hearted, very plain and sincere, without any suspicion or any malice in his nature.

Falling in love with a young girl-neighbour, he had demanded and obtained her hand. He was doing a tolerably fair dry-goods business, was making considerable money, and never supposed for a moment that the young girl had not accepted him for his own sake.

Besides she made him very happy. He did not believe there was any other woman in the world; he thought of no one but her; he gazed at her perpetually with eyes of adoration—prostrate adoration. At meal-times he was apt to do a thousand clumsy things in order not to lose a single moment's opportunity of looking at his darling's face: Sometimes he would pour wine in his plate, or pour water into the salt-cellar, and then laugh like a child, exclaiming:

"See, I love you too much: it makes me do a heap of foolish things."

She would smile, with an air of calm and resignation, and

then turn her eyes away as if wearied by her husband's idolatry, and she would try to make him talk about something, about anything, no matter what; but he would reach out and take her hand across the table, and keep pressing it in his own, murmuring:

"My little Jeanne,—my darling little Jeanne!"

She would become impatient at last, and exclaim:

"Come, now!—have some sense!—eat, and let me have a chance to eat."

Then he would sigh, break a mouthful of bread, and eat it slowly.

For five years they had had no children. Then, at last, a happy probability that she would soon become a mother made him almost delirious with joy. He remained continually in his wife's company,—so much so, in fact, that his housekeeper, the good old woman who had brought him up, and who exercised a certain amount of authority over him, would fairly push him out of the house sometimes, and shut the door on him, in order to compel him to take a little fresh air.

An intimate friendship had long been established between himself and a young man who had known his wife from a child, and who held the position of assistant superintendent in the office of the Prefecture. M. Duretour dined at M. Lemonnier's house three times a week, used to bring flowers to Mme. Lemonnier, and sometimes tickets for the theatre; and often, during dessert, good Lemonnier would exclaim with feeling, turning to his wife:

"With a companion such as you and a friend like him, one can feel assured of being perfectly happy in this world."

She died in childbed. He almost died also from the shock. But the sight of the child gave him courage,—a tiny little moaning creature.

He loved it with a passionate and painful love,—a suffering love blended with memory of his loss,—but a love in which there survived something of his adoration for the dear dead woman. That child was the flesh of his wife, a continuation of her being: something like a quintessence of herself. That child was her own very life, inclosed in another body: she had passed away only that he might live. . . . And the father would kiss him wildly. . . . But then he would also think that child had killed her,—had taken away, stolen, the idolized life, —was nourished by it,—had absorbed her rightful share of existence. And M. Lemonnier would put the child in the cradle, and sit down to look at him. He would sit there for hours and hours at a time, watching him, dreaming over a thousand sad or sweet recollections. Then, while the little one slept, he would bend over him and weep,—letting his tears fall on the baby's face.

*　　*　　*　　*　　*　　*　　*

The child grew up. The father could scarcely resign himself to pass a single hour away from him: he kept always around him, took him out walking, dressed and washed him with his own hands, fed him. His friend, M. Duretour, also seemed very fond of the little fellow, and would kiss him sometimes with just such bursts of affection as parents show. He would jump him up in his arms, and ride him on his knee for hours at a time, and lift up his little dress to kiss his fat little legs. Then M. Lemonnier would exclaim delightedly:

"Isn't he a darling?—isn't he a darling?"

And M. Duretour would hug the child closely, and tickle his neck with the hairs of his moustache.

Céleste, the old housekeeper, was the only one who appeared to have no fondness for the child. She used to be very angry at the mischief he did about the house, and seemed exasperated at the manner in which the two men petted him. She would cry out:

"Is that the way for anybody to raise a child? You're just going to make a horrid monkey out of him!" . . .

Time passed, and Jean became nine years old. He could scarcely read at all, they had spoiled him so much; and he never did anything except what he pleased. He had a tenacious self-will, obstinate powers of resistance, frenzied fits of temper. The father always yielded,—gave in to every whim. M. Duretour was continually buying and bringing toys which the child asked for; and he fairly fed him on cakes and candies.

Then Céleste grew furious, and screamed out:

"It is a shame, sir!—it is just a shame! You are ruining that child—just ruining him, do you hear? . . . But this thing will have to stop, sooner or later;—yes, yes, it's got to stop, I tell you;—I promise you it's got to stop, and that before long, too!"

M. Lemonnier answered smilingly:

"How can I help it, my good woman?—I love him too much; I don't know how to refuse him anything, and you must really try to love him too."

*   *   *   *   *   *   *

Jean was weakly,—slightly sick. The doctor declared it a case of anemia,—ordered iron, rare meat, and beef-soup.

Now it happened that the child liked nothing but cakes and refused all other food; and the father, in despair, stuffed him with cream-tarts and chocolate candy.

One evening, as they sat opposite each other at table, Céleste brought in the soup-dish with an air of assurance and authority—such as she very seldom assumed. She took off the cover brusquely, pitched the ladle into the vessel, and exclaimed:

"There's the very best soup I ever made you;—the little one's got to eat some of it this time!"

M. Lemonnier bowed his head in consternation. He felt that a storm was brewing.

Céleste seized his plate, filled it herself, and placed it before him.

He tasted the soup at once, and observed:

"Yes, indeed,—it is really excellent!"

Then the housekeeper took the child's plate, and poured a ladle-full of soup into it. Then she retired two paces back, and waited.

Jean smelled the soup, pushed away the plate, and uttered

a *"phew"* of disgust. Céleste, turning pale, suddenly came forward, and seizing the spoon, forced it, full of soup, right into the child's half-opened mouth.

He choked, coughed, sneezed, spat, and, with a yell, seized his glass and flung it at the old housekeeper. It struck her full in the stomach. Then in exasperation she took the little brat's head under her arm, and commenced to poke spoonful after spoonful of soup down his throat by main force. He vomited them as fast as they went down, stamped, writhed, choked, beat the air with his hands, and turned so red that he looked as if he was going to die.

At first the father remained so much surprised that he did not make a single movement. Then, all of a sudden, he leaped at the housekeeper with the rage of a madman, seized her by the throat, and hurled her against the wall. He stammered:

"Out of here! . . . out! . . . out, you beast!"

But she flung him from her with a sudden effort; and then, all disheveled, her cap fallen upon her shoulders, and her eyes aflame, she screamed:

"Are you going crazy now? You want to beat me because I make the child take soup,—the child you are just spoiling to death!"

He repeated, shaking from head to foot:

"Out of here!" . . . get out,—get out, you brute!"

Then in fury she advanced upon him, and looking right into his eyes, with her voice all trembling, she cried:

"Ah! you think . . . you think you are going to treat me

like that . . . me, me? . . . Ah! indeed no! . . . And for what, for what . . . for that brat that doesn't even belong to you? . . . No!—doesn't belong to you! . . . No!—doesn't belong to you! . . . doesn't belong to you! . . . doesn't belong to you! . . . Yes, and everybody knows it—everybody, except you! . . . Yes!—ask the grocer, ask the butcher, ask the baker, ask anybody—anybody!" . . .

She stammered and choked with anger;—then stopped, and looked at him.

He did not move. His face was livid; his arms hung down lifelessly. After a moment or two, he stuttered out, in a changed and trembling voice, but a voice rendered terrible by emotion:

"You say? . . . you say? . . . What is that you say?"

She remained silent, frightened by the look of his face. He took another step toward her, repeating:

"You say? . . . What is that you say?" . . .

Then in a calm tone she replied:

"I say just what I know—just what everybody knows!"

He lifted both hands, and flinging himself upon her in a fit of brutal rage, tried to hurl her to the floor. But she was strong, although old, and she was active also. She broke away from his clutch, and running away from him around the table, once more made furious, she yelped at him:

"Look at him—look at him, fool that you are!—look at him, and see if that is not the living image of M. Duretour! Why, look at his nose and his eyes: have you got that kind of eyes, and that kind of a nose? And his hair?—was her hair like that?—her hair—was it? I tell you everybody knows it,—everybody except you! It's the joke of the whole town! Look at him!" . . .

She reached the door, opened it, and disappeared.

Jean, utterly terrified, sat motionless in front of his soup-plate.

*   *   *   *   *   *   *

An hour after, she came back, very quietly—to look. The child,—after having eaten all the cakes, the cream, and the preserved pears,—was now devouring the contents of the jam-pot with his soup-spoon.

The father had gone out.

Céleste took the child, kissed him, and carried him on tip-toe to her room, where she put him to bed. And she went back to the dining-room, cleared the table, and set everything in order—feeling all the while very uneasy.

No sound could be heard in the house—none whatever. She went to her master's room, and put her ear against the door. He was not making any movement. She peeped through the keyhole. He was writing, and seemed tranquil.

Then she returned to her kitchen, and sat down waiting,— prepared for anything to happen; for she felt something was going to occur.

She fell asleep in her chair, and did not wake up before daylight.

She did the housework, just as she had been accustomed

to do, every morning; she swept out the rooms, dusted, and about eight o'clock made M. Lemonnier's coffee.

But she did not venture to carry it up to her master,—for she could not tell how she might be received; and she resolved to wait till he should ring the bell. He did not ring. Nine o'clock struck—then ten.

Céleste, feeling scared, prepared her tray, and went up-stairs with a beating heart. She paused before the door—listened. Nothing was moving inside. She rapped;—there was no response. Then, summoning up all her courage, she opened the door, entered,—and, with an awful cry, let fall the breakfast she was carrying.

M. Lemonnier was hanging there in the middle of the room, —suspended by a rope around his neck from the chandelier-ring of the ceiling. His tongue protruded hideously. His right slipper had fallen off, and was lying on the floor. The left was still on his foot. A chair, kicked over, had been flung as far as the bed. . . .

Céleste, horrified, fled away shrieking. All the neighbours ran in. The doctor found that death must have occurred about midnight.

A letter addressed to M. Duretour was found upon the table. It contained only this line:

"I leave and confide the child to you."

TWO FRIENDS

TWO FRIENDS

Paris was blockaded,—famished,—at her last gasp. The sparrows were becoming very rare upon the roofs, and the sewers were losing their population of rats. People ate anything they could get.

As he was trudging sadly along the exterior boulevard, one fine January morning, with his stomach empty,—his hands thrust into the pockets of his uniform trousers, M. Morissot, watchmaker by trade, stopped short in face of a man whom he recognized as a friend. It was M. Sauvage, whose acquaintance he had made while angling.

Before the war, every Sunday at dawn, M. Morissot used to start out with a bamboo fishing-rod in his hand, and a tin box strapped to his back. He would take the Argenteuil train, get out at Colombes, and walk to l'Ile Marante. On reaching this scene of his dreams he would at once begin fishing, and would keep on fishing until nightfall.

Every Sunday also he used to meet there a little pursy, jolly man,—M. Sauvage,—dry goods dealer in the Rue Notre Dame de Lorette,—another fanatical angler. They would often sit there a whole half-day, side by side,—line in hand and feet dangling over the current; and they had conceived a great friendship for one another.

Some days they did not talk. Occasionally they might drop a word or two; but they understood each other admirably well, without saying anything,—having similar tastes and identical ideas.

Of a spring morning, about ten o'clock, when the rejuvenated sun would be creating that light mist which flows away with the water, and would be pouring down on the backs of the two enthusiastic fishers the pleasant warmth of the new season —then would Morissot sometimes say to his neighbour "Hey! —this is fine, isn't it?" And M. Sauvage would answer: "Don't know of anything finer!" And that sufficed them for comprehending and esteeming each other.

Toward the end of an autumn day, when the sky, all ensanguined by sunset, would be flinging upon the water shapes of scarlet cloud,—would be purpling the whole river, setting fire to the heavens, reddening the faces of the two friends, and gilding the already fading foliage, as it trembled with the first shivers of winter,—then M. Morissot would look at M. Sauvage with a smile and say: "What a sight!" And M. Sauvage, delighted, would answer, without taking his eyes off his float: "This is better than the boulevard,—eh?"

*   *   *   *   *   *   *

The moment they recognized each other, they shook hands energetically,—quite affected to find themselves together under such a changed condition of affairs. M. Sauvage murmured with a sigh:

"Here's a nice state of things!" Morissot, very gloomy,

groaned out: "And such weather!—to-day is the first fine day of the year."

The sky was, in fact, quite blue, and full of light.

They began to walk along, side by side, sad and dreamy. Morissot spoke again: "And that fishing,—eh?—what a fine time we had then!"

M. Sauvage asked:

"When shall we ever have such another?"

They entered a little café, and took an absinthe together: they then went out to walk about the boulevards again.

Morissot suddenly stopped: "Let's take another—eh?" M. Sauvage consented:—"Just as you like." And they went into another drinking-resort.

They felt quite dizzy when they came out, and trembled, as people do who have swallowed plenty of alcohol upon an empty stomach. It was pleasant outside. A mild breeze caressed their faces.

M. Sauvage, made quite tipsy by the warm air, stopped and said:

"Suppose we go, anyhow?"

"Go where?"

"Why, to fish, of course."

"But where?"

"Why, to our old place—the island. The French outposts are at Colombes. I know Colonel Dumoulin; he'll pass us through all right."

Morissot trembled with desire. "Good!" he cried:—"I'll go!" And they went off to get their fishing-tackle.

An hour later they were walking along the high-road, side by side. Then they reached the villa where the Colonel was. He smiled at their whim, and gave his consent at once. They walked on, provided with a written permit.

In a short time they passed beyond the outposts, traversed deserted Colombes, and found themselves at the edge of the little vineyards which slope down to the Seine. It was about eleven o'clock.

The village of Argenteuil in front of them seemed dead. The heights of Orgemont and Sannois dominated the landscape. The great plain which reaches to Nanterre was empty —perfectly bare,—with its naked cherry-trees and gray fields.

M. Sauvage, pointing to the heights, said: "The Prussians are there!" And a sense of uneasiness almost paralyzed the two friends as they gazed upon the deserted country.

"The Prussians!" They had never seen them; but they *felt them* there, as they had felt their presence for two long months around Paris,—ruining France, pillaging, massacring, starving-out the people,—invisible and omnipotent enemies. And a sort of superstitious terror blended itself with their hatred of those unknown and victorious people.

Morissot stammered:—"Say! . . . suppose, suppose we'd meet some of them?"

M. Sauvage replied, with that peculiar Parisian *gouaillerie,*

—that spirit of jest which will crop out under any possible circumstances:

"Why, we'd just offer them some nice broiled fish."

Nevertheless they hesitated to go further on—feeling intimidated by the silence of the whole horizon.

At last M. Sauvage decided:—"Come, let us go—but prudently." And they descended a vineyard slope, bending down, crouching on all fours, taking advantage of every bush to screen themselves as they advanced, straining their ears, and looking anxiously around.

A narrow strip of bare land remained to cross in order to reach the river bank. They started at a run, and as soon as they got to the shore, they crouched down among the reeds.

Morissot put his ear to the ground in order to find out if somebody was not walking about in the neighbourhood. He could not hear anything. They were all alone,—quite by themselves.

They took courage and began to fish.

*   *   *   *   *   *   *

In front of them l'Ile Marante, now deserted, concealed them from observation from the further bank. The little restaurant was closed,—looked as if it had been closed for years and years.

M. Sauvage caught the first gudgeon;—M. Morissot the second; and then, moment by moment, they kept on lifting their lines, each time with some little silver creature quivering at the end of them—a really marvelous catch.

They carefully dropped the fish into a fishing-bag of strong close network, which lay in the shallow water at their feet. And a delicious joy penetrated them—such a joy as you feel on once more obtaining some loved pleasure of which you had been long deprived.

The kind sun poured down his warmth between their shoulders; they ceased to hear anything; they thought of nothing more; they ignored the rest of the world;—they simply fished!

But suddenly a deep sound that seemed to rise out of the ground made everything shake. The cannon were at work again.

Morissot turned his head, and above the slope he saw, high on the right, the great silhouette of Mont Valerien, bearing on its brow a white plume,—a puff of powder-smoke.

And immediately a second jet of smoke puffed out from the summit of the fortress;—a few seconds later, the detonation came to their ears.

Then other reports followed; and from time to time the mountain exhaled its breath of destruction, blew forth milky vapors, which rose in the clear sky to hang as a cloud above it.

M. Sauvage shrugged his shoulders:

"There they go!" he said.

Morissot, who was watching the feather on his float dipping again and again, was suddenly seized with the wrath that a peaceful man feels, against the people who were fighting thus; and he muttered between his teeth:

"What idiots!—to be killing one another like that!"

M. Sauvage answered:

"Worse than brutes."

And Morissot, who had just hooked a whitebait, exclaimed: "Just to think it will always be like that as long as there are governments!"

M. Sauvage interrupted him:

"The Republic would not have declared war——"

M. Morissot interrupted in his turn: "With kings there is foreign war; with a Republic, civil war."

And very calmly they proceeded to discuss politics,—unraveling great problems with the healthy reasoning of gentle and plainly educated men,—both agreeing on one point, that humanity would never be free. And Mont Valerien thundered on without a pause,—demolishing French houses with solid shot, braying out lives, crushing beings—puttings an end to many dreams, many anticipated joys, many a hope of bliss; —opening in the hearts of wives and in the hearts of daughters, and in the hearts of mothers, dwelling far away in other lands, wounds that would never heal.

"Such is life!" declared M. Sauvage.

"Better say, such is death!" responded Morissot with a laugh.

But they suddenly started in terror,—feeling that somebody was walking behind them; and, turning round to look, they saw, right at their backs, four men,—four tall bearded men, armed, dressed like livery servants, and wearing flat caps, who were covering them with rifles.

The two fishing-lines slipped from their hands, and went floating down the river.

In an instant the two Parisians were seized, tied, dragged away, pitched into a boat, and taken to the island beyond.

And behind the house which they had imagined deserted, they saw a company of some twenty German soldiers.

A sort of hairy giant, who, seated a-straddle of a chair, was smoking a big porcelain pipe, asked them, in excellent French:

"Well, gentlemen, was the fishing good?"

Then a soldier threw down at the officer's feet the net-full of fish, which he had taken good care to bring along. The Prussian smiled: "Well, well!—I see you had pretty good luck. . . . But we have something else to talk about now. Listen to me, and don't feel uneasy.

"In my opinion, you are simply two spies sent to watch me. I take you, therefore, and have you shot at once. You were pretending to fish, just so as to conceal your real designs. You have fallen now into my hands. So much the worse for you;—war is war!

"But as you must have passed the outposts, you must also certainly have a password in order to get back. Give me that pass-word, and I shall let you go!"

The two friends, standing side by side, with faces livid, and hands quivering a little from nervous excitement, answered not a word.

The officer resumed: "No one shall ever know; you can

return home quietly. The secret will disappear with you. If you refuse, it's death—and that immediately. Choose!"

They remained motionless, without uttering a syllable.

The Prussian, always perfectly cool, pointed to the river, and continued:

"Think of it!—in five minutes you will be at the bottom of that water. In five minutes! You must have relatives."

And still Mont Valerien uttered its thunder.

The two fishers remained silent. The German gave orders in his own language. Then he moved his chair back, so as not to be too close to the prisoners; and twelve men took their places in line twenty paces off, with rifles at attention.

The officer spoke again.

"I give you one minute—not a second more."

Then he rose up suddenly, approached Morissot, led him away by the arm to a short distance, and said to him in a whisper: "Quick! tell me that password. Your comrade will know nothing about it. I'll just pretend to have changed my mind, to take pity on you."

Morissot made no reply.

The Prussian led M. Sauvage away, and put the same question to him.

M. Sauvage made no reply.

The two friends found themselves side by side once more.

And the officer gave the word of command;—the soldiers brought up their rifles to a present.

Then the eyes of Morissot fell upon the net full of fish, lying there in the grass, a few steps away from him.

A beam of sunlight made the heap of fish glimmer, as they still quivered. And he felt weak for the first time. In spite of all his efforts, the tears rose to his eyes.

He stammered out:

"Goodby, M. Sauvage."

M. Sauvage replied:

"Goodby, M. Morissot."

They shook hands, shaking from head to foot with a trembling they could not master.

The officer gave the word,—"Fire!"

The twelve shots made only one report.

M. Sauvage fell all of a heap on his nose. Morissot, a taller man, swayed, twirled, and fell back across his comrade, with his face to the sky,—while thick gushes of blood escaped from his vest,—all burst in at the breast.

Again the German gave some orders.

His men scattered, and came back with ropes and some big stones, which they fastened to the feet of the two dead men. Then they carried them to the river-bank.

Mont Valerien still roared,—now coiffed with a mountain of smoke.

Two soldiers took Morissot by the head and by the legs; —two others lifted Sauvage in the same way. The corpses, strongly swung a moment, were flung far out in a curve, and fell, feet foremost, into the river,—the weight of the stones dragging down the feet first.

The water splashed, bubbled, quivered;—then calmed down, while two little waves broke against the shore.

A little blood floated away.

The officer, always serene, muttered: "The fishes' turn now!"

Then he walked back to the house.

And suddenly he perceived the net full of gudgeons in the grass. He lifted it, looked at it, smiled, and called out:

"Wilhelm!"

A soldier, wearing a white apron, ran out.

And the Prussian, flinging to him the catch of the two dead men, ordered:

"Cook for me these little things right off—fry them while they are still alive. They will make a delicious dish."

Then he resumed his pipe.

A PARRICIDE

A PARRICIDE

The counsel for the defense had pleaded insanity. How could so strange a crime, he asked, be otherwise explained.

Among the reeds near Chatou, two dead bodies had been found one morning, with their arms twined about each other,—a man and woman, both well-known members of fashionable society, rich, not young, and married only the year before—the lady having been three years a widow.

They were not known to have had any enemies;—the bodies had not been robbed. It appeared that they had both been stabbed with some long pointed instrument, and then flung from the bank into the river.

The inquest had not brought out any fresh facts. The boatmen of the neighbourhood were questioned in vain; and the authorities were on the point of abandoning the investigation, when a young cabinet-maker of the neighbouring village, named George Louis, and nicknamed *"Le Bourgeois,"* voluntarily gave himself up as the murderer.

In reply to various questions asked, he answered only this:

"I knew the man for two years; I knew the woman only for six months past. They used often to come to get me to mend old furniture for them, because I am a good hand at the business."

And when they asked him:

"What did you kill them for?"

He replied obstinately:

"I killed them because I wanted to kill them."

Nothing further could be got out of him.

The man was of illegitimate birth no doubt;—as a child he had been first left in care of a paid nurse in the country, and had been subsequently abandoned by his parents. He had no other real name than George Louis; but, as he grew up, he proved to be a remarkably intelligent boy, with naturally fine tastes and good manners, and his comrades had therefore nicknamed him *"Le Bourgeois,"* by which name alone, he became subsequently known. He had the reputation of being remarkably skilful at the trade of cabinet-maker which he had adopted. He was even able to do some wood-carving. He was also said to be very excitable in his disposition,—a believer in Communistic, and even in Nihilistic doctrines,— a great reader of sensational novels and tragical light-litera- ture,—also a man of some influence at elections, and a first- rate stump orator at workingmen's meetings or political gath- erings of farmers.

*   *   *   *   *   *   *

The counsel for the defense had pleaded insanity.

How, indeed, was it possible to suppose that this workman could have knowingly killed his best customers,—rich and generous customers, as the prisoner himself had admitted,— customers who had given him more than three thousand francs' worth of work to do in the last three years (there were his books to prove it)? There was only one explanation possible:—insanity—the insanity caused by the long haunting of one persistent idea,—the idea of the *déclassé*, the man who deems himself a social outcast, and who avenges himself on two *bourgeois* of all the *bourgeois*. Here the lawyer made a skilful allusion to the nickname of *"Le Bourgeois,"* given by the country-people to this foundling; and he cried out:

"Is not the very name an irony, and an irony well calculated to intensify still more the nervous exaltation of this fatherless and motherless boy? He is an ardent Republican. Nay!— what do I say? He belongs to that very same political party which the Republic shot down or transported for life in former days, but to which she opens her welcoming arms to-day —the party of those with whom incendiarism is a principle, and murder the most ordinary of political methods.

"Those atrocious doctrines,—publicly proclaimed to-day at mass-meetings,—are the cause of this man's ruin. He heard Republicans,—yes, he even heard women, women!—clamour for the blood of M. Gambetta, and for the blood of M. Grévy; —his ill-balanced mind capsized under the shock;—a thirst for blood came upon him—a thirst for the blood of the *bourgeois!*

"It is not this man who should be condemned: it is the Commune!"

Murmurs of applause passed through the courtroom. Everybody felt that the counsel for the defense had won his case. The counsel for the prosecution did not even make an attempt to reply.

Then the Judge put the usual formal question to the accused:

"Prisoner, do you wish to say anything further in your own behalf?"

The man got up. He was of low stature and frail aspect, with flaxen-fair hair, and bright, steady, gray eyes. A powerful, frank, and sonorous voice burst from the chest of the slender youth; and immediately,—with the utterance of his very first words,—entirely changed the opinion that the audience had previously formed of him.

He spoke loudly, and in a declamatory manner, but so clearly that every syllable was plainly audible even at the further end of the vast courtroom:

"Your Honor, as I do not wish to be placed in a madhouse, and as I would prefer even the guillotine, I am going to tell you all about this affair.

"I killed that man and that woman because they were my parents.

"Now, listen to me, and judge me.

"A woman was secretly delivered of a son and sent him far away, somewhere, to a professional nurse. Did she even know whither her accomplice bore the little innocent creature —innocent, yet doomed to endless misery, to the shame of illegitimate birth, to worse than all that—to death, since he was abandoned, since the nurse, failing to receive the monthly stipend, might, as nurses often do, let the child waste away, suffer from hunger, die from neglect?

"The woman who nursed me was honest—more honest, more noble, more of a woman, more of a mother than my own mother. She brought me up. She erred in thus doing her duty. Better far to leave such children to perish,—such miserable foundlings cast away at the outskirts of villages, even as refuse is dumped beyond the limits of towns!

"I grew up with a vague idea that I bore the brand of a disgrace. The other children called me '*bâtard*' one day. They did not know what the word meant,—one of them having that day heard it uttered for the first time by his parents. I did not know what it meant, either—but I felt it.

"I may state that I was one of the most intelligent boys in the school. I would have been an upright man, your Honor, —perhaps a man above the common run,—if my parents had not committed the crime of abandoning me.

"That crime was committed against me. I was the victim; —they were the criminals. I was helpless;—they were pitiless. They ought to have loved me;—they flung me from them.

"I owed them life—but is life a gift? Mine, at all events, was simply a curse. After their shameful abandonment of me, I owed them nothing but revenge. They perpetrated against me the most inhuman, the most infamous, the most monstrous act which it is possible to commit against a human being.

"The man who is cursed at strikes back; the man who is

robbed seeks to wrest back from the robber by force that which belongs to him. The man who is duped, mocked, martyrized, kills;—the man who has his face slapped in public, kills;—the man who is dishonored, kills. I have been worse robbed, worse duped, worse martyrized, worse insulted and dishonored morally, than any one of those whose anger you might condone.

"I have avenged myself; I have killed. That was my legitimate right! I took their life, their happy life away, in exchange for that hideous life which they had imposed upon me.

"You can talk of parricide! Were they even to be considered my parents—those people by whom I was regarded merely as an abominable burden, a terror, a load of infamy—those people for whom my birth was a calamity, and my life a perpetual menace of shame? They sought only their own egotistical will;—they had a child they did not want. They suppressed that child. And my turn came at last to suppress them likewise!

"And, neverthelses, it is only a little while ago that I was ready to love them.

"About two years ago, as I have already told you, the man who was my father entered my shop for the first time. I had no suspicions then. He ordered two articles of furniture made. He had previously—as I afterward learned,—made inquiries about me of the parish priest, under promise of secrecy, as you may well imagine.

"He came back often,—gave me plenty of work to do, and paid me well. Sometimes he would even converse with me about this topic, or that topic—different things. I felt an affectionate regard for him.

"About the commencement of this year, he brought to my place, for the first time, his wife—my mother. When she came in, she trembled so much that I at first supposed her to be afflicted with some nervous disease. Then she asked for a chair, and a glass of water. She said nothing;—she stared at my furniture like a crazy woman; and when he asked her anything she could only answer 'Yes,' 'No,' at random. By the time she left I had begun to think that her mind was slightly affected.

"She came again the following month. That time she was calm and self-possessed. They gave me quite a large order, and chatted with me for a considerable time. I saw her three times more after that without suspecting anything; but, lo and behold! one day she began to question me about my life, about my childhood, about my parents! 'Madame,' I said, 'my parents were miserable wretches who disowned me.' When I said that, she pressed her hand over her heart, and fell senseless on the floor. I thought to myself at once,—'That is my mother!'—but I knew better than to betray myself. I waited to see her come again.

"You may be sure I made inquiries. I learned they had only been married the July before;—my mother had then been a widow three years. There were whispered rumours that they had loved during the lifetime of the husband; but there was no proof. I, I was the proof—the proof they had begun by hiding, and had afterward hoped to destroy.

"I waited. She came again one evening, accompanied, as usual, by my father. That day she seemed to be very much affected—I do not know why. Then, just as she was going away, she turned and said to me:—'I wish you well, because you appear to be a good young man, an industrious one. You will be thinking about getting married one of these days;— I want to help you to choose for yourself a wife that you know will suit you. I myself was once married against my will; and I know how much suffering an unfortunate match may cause. Now I am free, without children, and rich, mistress of my own fortune. Here is your dowry.'

"She handed me a big sealed envelope.

"I looked at her very hard;—I said to her:

"'*You are my mother?*'

"She shrank back a little, and hid her face with her hands, so as not to see me. He—the man—my father,—caught her in his arms, and shouted at me:

"'Why, you must be crazy!'

"I answered: 'Not a bit! I know you two are my parents. You cannot fool me that way. Confess the truth, and I will keep your secret;—I will have no ill-will against you; I will remain just what I am—a cabinet-maker.'

"He moved back toward the door, supporting his wife in

his arms;—she was sobbing. I rushed to the door, locked it, put the key in my pocket, and said again:

"'Look at her and dare to deny again that she is my mother!'

"Then he lost his temper, turned white,—terrified at the idea that the scandal which had been so long hushed up might burst out all of a sudden,—that their position, their honor would all be lost at once; he stuttered out:

"'You are a villain trying to blackmail us! . . . This is what comes of trying to do good to the people—trying to help and befriend clowns and brutes.'

"My mother, completely overwhelmed, could only cry out, over and over again:

"'Oh! let us get out of here!—let us get out!'

"Then, as the door was still locked, he cried:

"'If you don't open this door at once, I'll have you arrested for assault and attempt to blackmail!'

"I still kept my temper; I opened the door, and watched them disappear in the darkness.

"Then, all of a sudden, it seemed to me that I had suddenly been made an orphan,—had been again abandoned—flung out into the gutter. A frightful oppression, mingled with anger, with hatred, with disgust, came upon me;—I felt within me something like an uprising of my very life,—an uprising in the name of justice, in the name of honor, in the name of truth, in the name of affection trampled upon. I ran to overtake them—along the bank of the Seine, which I knew they would have to follow in order to reach the railroad station of Chatou.

"I came up with them very soon. The night had become perfectly black. I walked stealthily through the grass, so that they could not hear me. My mother was still crying. My father said:—'It was all your fault. Why did you insist on seeing him? It was simply madness for people in our position to do such a thing. We could have done him all the good imaginable, without showing ourselves at all. Since we cannot possibly recognize him, what was the use of making those dangerous visits?'

"Then I leaped right in front of them, and supplicated. I stammered out:—'You know very well you are my parents! —you have rejected me once; will you now repel me a second time?'

"Then, your honour, he raised his hand against me!—he did!—I swear it by my manhood, by the law, by the Republic! He struck me!—and when I took him by the neck, he pulled a revolver out of his pocket!

"I saw everything red that moment,—don't know how it happened;—I had my compass in my pocket, and I struck him with it—struck him as hard as I could, and as many times as I could.

"Then she began to scream, 'Help! murder!'—and pull out my beard. . . . It seems I killed her too. How do I know what I did in that moment?

"Then, when I saw them both lying there, dead,—I pitched them into the Seine, without reflection.

"That is all. . . . Now, judge me!"

*   *   *   *   *   *   *

The prisoner resumed his seat. In view of this revelation, the case was held over to be tried at the next session. It will soon come up. If we were on the jury what would we do with this parricide?

THE JEWELRY

THE JEWELRY

HAVING met the girl one evening, at the house of the office-superintendent, M. Lantin became enveloped in love as in a net.

She was the daughter of a country-tutor, who had been dead for several years. Afterward she had come to Paris with her mother, who made regular visits to several *bourgeois* families of the neighbourhood, in hopes of being able to get her daughter married. They were poor and respectable, quiet and gentle. The young girl seemed to be the very ideal of that pure good woman to whom every young man dreams of entrusting his future. Her modest beauty had a charm of angelic shyness; and the slight smile that always dwelt about her lips seemed a reflection of her heart.

Everybody sang her praises; all who knew her kept saying: "The man who gets her will be lucky. No one could find a nicer girl than that."

M. Lantin, who was then chief clerk in the office of the Minister of the Interior, with a salary of 3,500 francs a year, demanded her hand, and married her.

He was unutterably happy with her. She ruled his home with an economy so adroit that they really seemed to live in luxury. It would be impossible to conceive of any attentions, tendernesses, playful caresses which she did not lavish upon her husband; and such was the charm of her person that, six years after he married her, he loved her even more than he did the first day.

There were only two points upon which he ever found fault with her,—her love of the theatre, and her passion for false jewelry.

Her lady-friends (she was acquainted with the wives of several small office holders) were always bringing her tickets for the theatres; whenever there was a performance that made a sensation, she always had her *loge* secured, even for first performances; and she would drag her husband with her to all these entertainments, which used to tire him horribly after his day's work. So at last he begged her to go to the theatre with some lady-acquaintances who would consent to see her home afterward. She refused for quite a while;—thinking it would not look very well to go out thus unaccompanied by her husband. But finally she yielded, just to please him; and he felt infinitely grateful to her therefor.

Now this passion for the theatre at last evoked in her the desire of dress. It was true that her toilette remained simple, always in good taste, but modest; and her sweet grace, her irresistible grace, ever smiling and shy, seemed to take fresh charm from the simplicity of her robes. But she got into the habit of suspending in her pretty ears two big cut pebbles, fashioned in imitation of diamonds; and she wore necklaces of false pearls, bracelets of false gold, and haircombs studded with paste-imitations of precious stones.

Her husband, who felt shocked by this love of tinsel and show, would often say:—"My dear, when one has not the means to afford real jewelry, one should appear adorned with one's natural beauty and grace only,—and these gifts are the rarest of jewels."

But she would smile sweetly and answer: "What does it matter? I like those things—that is my little whim. I know you are right; but one can't make oneself over again. I've always loved jewelry so much!"

And then she would roll the pearls of the necklaces between her fingers, and make the facets of the cut crystals flash in the light, repeating: "Now look at them—see how well the work is done. You would swear it was real jewelry."

He would then smile in his turn, and declare to her: "You have the tastes of a regular Gipsy."

Sometimes, in the evening, when they were having a chat by the fire, she would rise and fetch the morocco box in which she kept her "stock" (as M. Lantin called it),—would put it on the tea-table, and begin to examine the false jewelry with passionate delight, as if she experienced some secret and mysterious sensations of pleasure in their contemplation; and she would insist on putting one of the necklaces round her husband's neck, and laugh till she couldn't laugh any more, crying out: "Oh! how funny you look!" Then she would rush into his arms, and kiss him furiously.

One winter's night, after she had been to the Opera, she came home chilled through, and trembling. Next day she had a bad cough. Eight days after that, she died of pneumonia.

Lantin was very nearly following her into the tomb. His despair was so frightful that in one single month his hair turned white. He wept from morning till night, feeling his heart torn by inexpressible suffering,—ever haunted by the memory of her, by the smile, by the voice, by all the charm of the dead woman.

Time did not assuage his grief. Often during office hours his fellow-clerks went off to a corner to chat about this or that topic of the day,—his cheeks might have been seen to swell up all of a sudden, his nose wrinkle, his eyes fill with water;—he would pull a frightful face, and begin to sob.

He had kept his dead companion's room just in the order she had left it, and he used to lock himself up in it every evening to think about her;—all the furniture, and even all her dresses, remained in the same place they had been on the last day of her life.

But life became hard for him. His salary, which, in his wife's hands, had amply sufficed for all household needs, now proved scarcely sufficient to supply his own few wants. And he asked himself in astonishment how she had managed always to furnish him with excellent wines and with delicate eating which he could not now afford at all with his scanty means.

He got a little into debt, like men obliged to live by their wits. At last one morning that he happened to find himself without a cent in his pocket, and a whole week to wait before

he could draw his monthly salary, he thought of selling something; and almost immediately it occurred to him to sell his
wife's "stock,"—for he had always borne a secret grudge
against the flash-jewelry that used to annoy him so much in
former days. The mere sight of it, day after day, somewhat spoiled the sad pleasure of thinking of his darling.

He tried a long time to make a choice among the heap of
trinkets she had left behind her;—for up to the very last day
of her life she had kept obstinately buying them, bringing
home some new thing almost every night;—and finally he
resolved to take the big pearl necklace which she used to like
the best of all, and which he thought ought certainly to be
worth six or eight francs, as it was really very nicely mounted
for an imitation necklace.

He put it in his pocket, and walked toward the office, following the boulevards, and looking for some jewelry-store on
the way, where he could enter with confidence.

Finally he saw a place and went in; feeling a little ashamed
of thus exposing his misery, and of trying to sell such a trifling
object.

"Sir," he said to the jeweler, "please tell me what this is
worth."

The jeweler took the necklace, examined it, weighed it,
took up a magnifying glass, called his clerk, talked to him in
whispers, put down the necklace on the counter, and drew
back a little bit to judge of its effect at a distance.

M. Lantin, feeling very much embarrassed by all these ceremonies, opened his mouth and began to declare:—"Oh! I know it can't be worth much" . . . when the jeweler interrupted him by saying:

"Well, sir, that is worth between twelve and fifteen thousand francs; but I cannot buy it unless you can let me know exactly how you came by it."

The widower's eyes opened enormously, and he stood gaping, —unable to understand. Then after a while he stammered out: "You said? . . . Are you sure?" The jeweler, misconstruing the cause of this astonishment, replied in a dry tone:— "Go elsewhere if you like, and see if you can get any more for it. The very most I would give for it is fifteen thousand. Come back and see me again, if you can't do better."

M. Lantin, feeling perfectly idiotic, took his necklace and departed; obeying a confused desire to find himself alone and to get a chance to think.

But the moment he found himself in the street again, he began to laugh, and he muttered to himself: "The fool!— oh! what a fool! If I had only taken him at his word. Well, well!—a jeweler who can't tell paste from real jewelry!"

And he entered another jewelry-store, at the corner of the Rue de la Paix. The moment the jeweler set eyes on the necklace, he exclaimed:—"Hello! I know that necklace well.— it was sold here!"

M. Lantin, very nervous, asked:

"What's it worth?"

"Sir, I sold it for twenty-five thousand francs. I am willing to buy it back again for eighteen thousand,—if you can prove to me satisfactorily, according to legal prescriptions, how you came into possession of it."—This time, M. Lantin was simply paralyzed with astonishment. He said: "Well . . . but please look at it again, sir. I always thought until now that it was . . . was false."

The jeweler said:

"Will you give me your name, sir?"

"Certainly. My name is Lantin; I am employed at the office of the Minister of the Interior. I live at No. 16, Rue des Martyrs."

The merchant opened the register, looked, and said: "Yes; this necklace was sent to the address of Madame Lantin, 16 Rue des Martyrs, on July 20th, 1876."

And the two men looked into each other's eyes;—the clerk wild with surprise; the jeweler suspecting he had a thief before him.

The jeweler resumed:

"Will you be kind enough to leave this article here for twenty-four hours only—I'll give you a receipt."

M. Lantin stuttered: "Yes—ah! certainly." And he went out, folding up the receipt, which he put in his pocket.

Then he crossed the street, went the wrong way, found out his mistake, returned by way of the Tuileries, crossed the Seine, found out he had taken the wrong road again, and went back to the Champs-Elysées without being able to get one clear idea into his head. He tried to reason, to understand. His wife could never have bought so valuable an object as that. Certainly not. But then, it must have been a present! . . . A present from whom? What for?

He stopped and stood stock-still in the middle of the avenue.

A horrible suspicion swept across his mind. . . . She? . . . But then all those other pieces of jewelry must have been presents also! . . . Then it seemed to him that the ground was heaving under his feet; that a tree, right in front of him, was falling toward him; he thrust out his arms instinctively, and fell senseless.

He recovered his consciousness again in a drug-store to which some bystanders had carried him. He had them lead him home, and he locked himself into his room.

Until nightfall he cried without stopping, biting his handkerchief to keep himself from screaming out. Then, completely worn out with grief and fatigue, he went to bed, and slept a leaden sleep.

A ray of sunshine awakened him, and he rose and dressed himself slowly to go to the office. It was hard to have to work after such a shock. Then he reflected that he might be able to excuse himself to the superintendent, and he wrote to him. Then he remembered he would have to go back to the jeweler's; and shame made his face purple. He remained thinking a long time. Still he could not leave the necklace there; he put on his coat and went out

It was a fine day; the sky extended all blue over the city,

and seemed to make it smile. Strollers were walking aimlessly about, with their hands in their pockets.

Lantin thought as he watched them passing: "How lucky the men are who have fortunes! With money a man can even shake off grief:—you can go where you please—travel,—amuse yourself! Oh! if I were only rich!"

He suddenly discovered he was hungry,—not having eaten anything since the evening before. But his pockets were empty; and he remembered the necklace. Eighteen thousand francs! Eighteen thousand francs!—that was a sum—that was!

He made his way to the Rue de la Paix and began to walk backward and forward on the sidewalk in front of the store. Eighteen thousand francs! Twenty times he started to go in; but shame always kept him back.

Still he was hungry—very hungry,—and had not a cent. He made one brusque resolve, and crossed the street almost at a run, so as not to let himself have time to think over the matter; and he rushed into the jeweler's.

As soon as he saw him, the merchant hurried forward, and offered him a chair with smiling politeness. Even the clerks came forward to stare at Lantin, with gayety in their eyes and smiles about their lips.

The jeweler said: "Sir, I made inquiries; and if you are still so disposed, I am ready to pay you down the price I offered you."

The clerk stammered: "Why, yes—sir, certainly.

The jeweler took from a drawer eighteen big bills, counted them, and held them out to Lantin, who signed a little receipt, and thrust the money feverishly into his pocket.

Then, as he was on the point of leaving, he turned to the ever-smiling merchant, and said, lowering his eyes: "I have some—I have some other jewelry, which came to me in the same—from the same inheritance. Would you purchase them also from me?"

The merchant bowed, and answered: "Why, certainly, sir—certainly. . . ." One of the clerks rushed out to laugh at his ease; another kept blowing his nose as hard as he could.

Lantin, impassive, flushed and serious, said: "I will bring them to you."

And he hired a cab to get the jewelry.

When he returned to the store, an hour later, he had not yet breakfasted. They examined the jewelry,—piece by piece,—putting a value on each. Nearly all had been purchased from that very house.

Lantin, now, disputed estimates made, got angry, insisted on seeing the books, and talked louder and louder the higher the estimates grew.

The big diamond earrings were worth 20,000 francs; the bracelets, 35,000; the brooches, rings, and medallions, 16,000; a set of emeralds and sapphires, 14,000; solitaire, suspended to a gold neckchain, 40,000; the total value being estimated at 196,000 francs.

The merchant observed with mischievous good nature: "The

person who owned these must have put all her savings into jewelry."

Lantin answered with gravity: "Perhaps that is as good a way of saving money as any other." And he went off, after having agreed with the merchant that an expert should make a counter-estimate for him the next day.

When he found himself in the street again, he looked at the Column Vendôme with the desire to climb it, as if it were a May pole. He felt jolly enough to play leapfrog over the Emperor's head,—up there in the blue sky.

He breakfasted at Voisin's restaurant, and ordered wine at 20 francs a bottle.

Then he hired a cab and drove out to the Bois. He looked at the carriages passing with a sort of contempt, and a wild desire to yell out to the passers-by: "I am rich, too—I am! I have 200,000 francs!"

The recollection of the office suddenly came back to him. He drove there, walked right into the superintendent's private room, and said: "Sir, I come to give you my resignation. I have just come into a fortune of *three* hundred thousand francs." Then he shook hands all round with his fellow-clerks; and told them all about his plans for a new career. Then he went to dinner at the Café Anglais.

Finding himself seated at the same table with a man who seemed to him quite genteel, he could not resist the itching desire to tell him, with a certain air of coquetry, that he had just inherited a fortune of *four* hundred thousand francs.

For the first time in his life he went to the theatre without feeling bored by the performance; and he passed the night in revelry and debauch.

Six months after he married again. His second wife was the most upright of spouses, but had a terrible temper. She made his life very miserable.

THE OLD MAN

THE OLD MAN

A WARM autumn sunlight was falling into the farmyard above the high beech trees bordering the road ditch. Under the grass, cropped short by the cows, the earth lay moist, impregnated with the recent rains, and yielded under the feet with a sloppy sound; and the burdened apple trees were scattering their pale green fruits through the deep green of the grass.

Four young heifers, tethered all in line, were grazing,— occasionally lifting their heads toward the farmhouse, and bleating;—about the manure-heap there was a great and brightly colored movement of fowls, before the stable—all scratching, pecking, and cackling; while the two cocks kept up a continuous crow, hunting worms for their hens, which they would call with a quick clucking noise.

The door of the wooden fence opened; a man came in,— perhaps forty years of age, but looking fully sixty,—wrinkled, crooked, taking long, slow steps encumbered by his heavy wooden shoes stuffed with straw. His disproportionately long arms hung down at either side as he walked. As he approached the farmhouse a yellow cur-dog, attached to the foot of an immense pear tree, close to the barrel, which served for a kennel, wagged his tail, and began to yelp for joy.

The man cried out:

"Down, Finot!"

The dog became quiet.

A peasant woman came out of the house. Her large, flat, bony body was sharply outlined under the woolen *caraco* which clung close to her figure. A gray skirt, too short for her, fell only half-way below her knees, over her blue woollen stockings; and she also wore wooden shoes stuffed with straw. A once white cap, that had become yellow with age, covered the scanty hair which still clung to her head; and her thin, brown, ugly toothless face had that wild-animal look which peasant faces so often wear.

The man asked:

"How's he doing?"

The woman replied:

"The priest says that's the last of him—that he won't get through the night."

They both entered the house.

After having passed through the kitchen, they entered the low black room, dimly lighted by a small square window before which hung a rag of Normandy calico. The big beams of the ceiling, darkened by time, all black and grimy, crossed overhead the whole length of the chamber, upholding the rickety floor of the attic, where bands of rats kept running about all day and all night.

The earthen floor, lumpy and wet, seemed greasy; and the bed made a dim white spot in the further end of the apart ment. A regular, hoarse sound—a sound of difficult, rattling, whistling breathing, with just such a gurgling as a broken pump makes,—came from the darkened bed where an old man was dying: the father of the peasant woman.

The man and woman approached, and looked at the agonizing man, with their placid and resigned gaze.

The son-in-law said:

"This time it's all up with him: he'll not even last till night."

The woman said:

"It's since midday that he's been gurgling like that."

Then they remained silent. The father's eyes were closed; his face had an earthen color, and looked so dry that it seemed made of wood. Through his half-open mouth the breath came hard and with a sound as of water lapping a bank; and the gray covering rose above his chest with every respiration.

After a long silence the son-in-law observed:

"Nothing to do now but let him go off quietly. I can't do anything for him. Anyhow it's unlucky for the crop: the weather's just right now, and we've got to transplant to-morrow."

This idea seemed to make the woman anxious. She reflected a little, and then said:

"Since he's going off now, we won't have to bury him before Saturday, and you'll have to-morrow for the planting."

The peasant thought awhile; he said:

"Yes, but to-morrow you see I'll have to be inviting for

the funeral;—it'll take me anyhow from five to six hours to go from Tourville to Manetôt and see all the folks."

The woman, after two or three moments' thinking, said:

"It's only three o'clock now; you can begin to get round before night, and you can call on all the folks at Tourville. You can just as well say that he's dead, since he can scarcely last till morning."

The man stood perplexed for a minute or two, comparing the advantages and consequences of this plan. Then he said:

"All right; I'm going."

He started toward the door, came back, and said, after a little hesitation:

"Seeing as you haven't anything else to do, you might as well peel some of them cooking apples, and make four dozen dumplings for the people who're coming to the funeral—as we've got to give them something. You can start the fire in the oven with that brushwood that's under the winepress shed. It's dry."

And he left the room, went to the kitchen, opened the cupboard, took a six-pound loaf, carefully cut off one slice, caught in the hollow of his hand all the crumbs that fell on the shelf, and poured them into his mouth so as not to lose any. Then with the tip of his knife he took a little salt butter from the bottom of a brown earthenware pot, and spread it over the bread, which he began to eat slowly,—like everything else he did.

And he passed through the yard again, quieted the dog,

who had again begun to whine, went out on the road which the farm ditch bordered, and disappeared in the direction of Tour- ville.

    *   *   *   *   *   *   *

Left alone, the woman set to work. She went to the flour barrel and began to make the paste for the dumplings. She kneaded it a long time, turning it over and over,—squeez- ing it, pressing it, braying it. Then she made one big yellowish- white ball of it, which she left on a corner of the table.

Then she went to get the apples; and for fear of injuring the tree with the pole, she climbed upon a stool. She picked out the fruit carefully, so as to get only the ripest, and put them into her apron.

A voice from the roadway called her:

"Hello, Madame Chicot!"

She turned round. It was one of their neighbours, Maître Osime Favet, the mayor, who was going to manure his lands, and sat with his legs hanging down over the side of his tumbril full of fertilizer. She answered:

"What can I do for you, Maître Osime?"

"The old man,—how's he doing?"

She screamed in answer:

"He's almost gone. The funeral's going to be on Saturday, at seven o'clock,—because we're in a hurry about the planting."

The neighbour replied:

"All right. Good luck! Take care of yourself."

She responded to his expression of good will:

"Thanks!—and you the same!"

Then she went on picking her apples.

As soon as she went into the house again, she resolved to take another look at her father, expecting to find him dead. But she had no sooner reached the door than she heard again the loud and monotonous rattling sound of his breathing; and deeming it useless to waste further time by going to the bed, she began to prepare the dumplings.

She enveloped each of the fruits, one by one, in a thin envelope of paste, and placed them in a row along the edge of the table. When she had made forty-eight dumplings—arranged by twelves, each row in front of the other,—she began to think about getting the supper ready, and hung the pot over the fire to cook the potatoes in; for she reflected that it would be no use to light the oven-fire that day, as she had the whole of the next day before her for the other preparations.

Her husband returned about five o'clock. As soon as he had crossed the threshold, he asked:

"Is he gone?"

She answered:

"Not yet—still gurgling away. . . ."

They went to look at him. The old man was in precisely the same condition as before. His hoarse breathing, regular as a clock-movement, had neither accelerated nor slackened. Every second it came,—varying slightly in tone, according as the air was leaving or entering the lungs.

His son-in-law stared at him and said:

"He'll end before we know it,—just like a candle going out."

They went back to the kitchen, and sat down to supper without speaking. When they had swallowed the soup, they ate a slice of bread-and-butter;—then, after the dishes had been washed, they went back to the dying man's room.

The wife, holding a little lamp with a smoking wick, held it before her father's face. If he had not been breathing they would certainly have supposed him dead.

The bed of the two peasants was hidden at the other end of the room,—in a sort of alcove. They went to bed without saying a word, blew out the light, closed their eyes; and in a short time two prolonged snorings,—one deeper, one shriller than the other,—sounded an accompaniment to the death-rattle of the dying man.

The rats were running in the attic.

*   *   *   *   *   *   *

The husband woke up with the first gleam of daylight. His step-father was still alive. He shook his wife,—feeling uneasy about the persistence of the old man in living.

"Say, Phémie,—he don't want to die at all! What ought we to do?—eh?"

He knew she had a good head for giving advice.

She answered:

"He'll never live through this day—sure! No fear of that! Then perhaps the mayor wouldn't object to us burying him to-morrow all the same—just as they buried old father Rénard, you know, that died just at sowing-time."

He was convinced by the force of her argument, and went to the fields right off.

His wife put her dumplings into the oven to cook, and did all the housework as usual.

At noon the old man was not yet dead. The men hired for the transplanting came in a group and looked at this old man who didn't want to die. Every man expressed his private opinion on the case;—then they all went to work.

At six o'clock, when the men came home, the father was still alive. The stepson got quite uneasy at last:

"What'll we do now, Phémie,—say?"

She was at a loss herself to know what to do. They went to see the mayor. The mayor promised to keep his eyes shut in the matter, and to authorize the burial for the next day. The health-officer, who was also seen, agreed to antedate the death-certificate, just to oblige Maître Chicot. Man and wife returned home with contented minds.

They went to bed and slept just as they had done the night before,—mingling the sound of their sonorous breathing with the feeble respiration of the old man.

When they woke up, he was not yet dead.

*   *   *   *   *   *   *

Then they were simply stupefied. They stood there beside the bed of the father,—looking at him with distrust, as if he had been trying to play them a mean trick,—to fool them,— to torment them just for fun; and they were especially vexed with him for causing them to lose so much time.

The son-in-law asked:

"What's to be done, now?"

She could not tell what to do;—she answered:

"Well, it's getting annoying, I must say!"

It was too late then to think of notifying all the persons invited, who were expected in a little while. Finally, it was resolved to wait for them, and explain the matter on their arrival.

About ten minutes to seven o'clock the first people came. The women all in black, with long veils over their heads, came in with sad faces. The men, feeling clumsy in their Sunday vests, came in with more assurance—two by two, chatting about their affairs.

Maître Chicot and his wife, quite bewildered, received them with many lamentations; and all at once, and at the same time, both began to weep as they advanced toward the visitors. They explained the affair, told how embarrassed they felt, brought out chairs, rushed here and there, made excuses, tried to prove to everybody that anybody else in their place would have had to do the same thing, and talked incessantly—becoming so loquacious all at once, that nobody else could get in a word.

They went from one guest to another, saying:

"I couldn't have believed it;—it's impossible to think how he could have lasted like that!"

The astonished mourners, feeling a little disconcerted—like all persons who miss an expected ceremony,—did not know what to do. Some sat down. Others remained standing. Some wanted to go back home; but Maître Chicot kept them, saying:

"We're going to take a bite of something, all the same. I made some dumplings—may as well eat them."

All the faces lighted up at this announcement. The folks began to chat in an undertone. The farm-yard gradually became full of people; and the first-comers told the news to the later arrivals. There was much whispering;—the thought of the dumplings made everybody feel good.

The women went in to look at the dying man. They crossed themselves when they came to the bed, muttered a prayer, and went out again. The men, less curious about such matters, simply glanced through the window which had been thrown open.

Madame Chicot explained the agony:

"It's two days now that he's been just like that—no better and no worse, no improvement and no falling off. . . . You'd think it was a pump with no more water,—wouldn't you?"

*   *   *   *   *   *   *

When everybody had taken a look at the dying man, all began to think about the lunch; but as there were too many people for all to go into the kitchen, the table was set out before the door. The four dozen dumplings, golden-yellow and very tempting, made their appearance in two big dishes, and attracted every eye. Each person reached out, and snatched at one, fearing there might not be enough to go round. But there were four over.

Maître Chicot, with his mouth full, observed:

"Say, if the old man could only see us now, he'd feel bad! I tell you he was the one who loved dumplings when he was alive."

A big jolly peasant answered:

"He'll never eat any more now. Every one in his turn."

This observation, far from casting any shade of gloom over the assembly, seemed to make every one merry. It was their turn,—to eat dumplings!

Madame Chicot—miserable at the pecuniary expense involved,—kept going to the cellar for cider. Jug succeeded jug, and was emptied almost as soon as brought. Then the folks began to laugh, to talk loud,—they even shouted, as they would shout at a party.

All at once an old peasant-woman, who had been retained at the bedside by the very fear of that fate which would certainly fall upon herself before long,—rushed to the window, and yelled out in a shrill voice:

"He's gone!—he's gone!"

Everybody hushed. The women jumped up at once to go and look.

He was indeed dead. The rattle had stopped in his throat. The men looked at each other, and then held their heads down, feeling uncomfortable. They had not yet finished chewing the dumplings. The old rascal had chosen to die just at the wrong time.

The Chicots had stopped weeping. Their minds were at rest: it was over now. They kept saying:

"Knew he couldn't last long like that. If he could only have died last night, we wouldn't be having all this trouble now."

No matter; it was over—anyhow! They would bury him on Monday—that was all there was about it; and there would be more dumplings cooked for the occasion.

The mourners went off chatting about the affair,—quite pleased to have been able to have seen such a thing, and eaten a snack.

And when the man and wife again found themselves alone, face to face, she said to him, with her face all contracted with anguish:

"Think I've now got to go and cook four dozen dumplings all over again! If he could only have died last night!"

But the husband, more patient, replied:

"Well, it isn't a thing you've got to do every day!"

THE ROBBER

THE ROBBER

"But when I tell you that nobody will believe it." . . .

"Never mind! But I feel obliged to assure you, to start with, that every word of what I'm going to tell you is true —however absurd it may seem. The only persons who could hear it without surprise are the painters,—especially the veteran artists who lived in the epoch of outlandish pranks and furious exaggerations,—that epoch when the spirit of fun was so strong that it would take possession of us under the most serious circumstances."

With this preamble the old artist bestraddled a chair, leaned his elbows upon the back of it, and began his narration.

We were all in the dining-room of a private residence at Barbizon.

He went on:—"Well, we had been having a dinner that evening at poor old Sorieul's,—you know Sorieul is dead now. He used to be the wildest fellow in the crowd. There were three of us that evening: Sorieul, myself, and Le Poittevin, I think;—but I could not now swear whether it was him or not. I mean the marine-painter, you know, Eugene Le Poittevin, who is now dead also,—not the landscape-painter, who is still alive and doing magnificent work.

"To say in those days that we had dined at Sorieul's was

215

equivalent to saying that we were all drunk. Le Poittevin was the only one who had kept his reason at all,—and though he was slightly tipsy, his wits were not gone. We were all of us very young in those times. We were lying down upon the rugs on the floor, in the little room which opened into the studio, and holding the most extravagant conversations imaginable. Sorieul, with his back on the floor, and his legs on a chair, was talking about battles, and the uniforms worn during the First Empire. All of a sudden he got up, and going to a big armoire where he kept his stock of costumes, took out a huzzar's uniform, and dressed himself in it. Then he wanted Le Poittevin to put on a grenadier's uniform. Le Poittevin resisted; so we seized him, stripped him by main force, and finally stuffed him into a uniform so big that he seemed to be swallowed up in it.

"I dressed up as a cuirassier. And Sorieul made us execute various complicated military movements. Finally he cried:—'Since we are all troopers to-night, let us drink like troopers.'

"We made a burnt-rum punch, swallowed it; and again filled the bowl with punch, and set fire to it. And we sang with all the force of our lungs the old troopers' songs,—the old-fashioned ditties which used to be trolled out by the soldiers of the old French armies.

"All of a sudden, Le Poittevin, who in spite of all the drinking, had been able to keep his head tolerably clear, made us hush; and after listening in silence for a second or two, he said in a whisper; *'I'm sure I heard some one walking in the studio.'* Sorieul rose to his feet as steadily as he could, and shouted: 'A robber!—what splendid luck.' Then, suddenly, he intoned the Marseillaise:

> " 'Aux armes, citoyens!'

"And rushing to a panoply he equipped us with weapons,— arming each man according to his uniform. I had a sabre and some kind of musket; Le Poittevin got a gigantic gun with a bayonet fixed to it; and Sorieul, not being able at once to find just what he wanted, seized a horse-pistol which he stuck into his belt, and brandished a sailor's ax. Then he cautiously opened the door of the studio; and the army invaded the suspicious territory beyond.

"When we found ourselves in the middle of the immense apartment,—all encumbered with vast canvasses, articles of furniture, extraordinary and fantastic objects of all sorts, Sorieul said:—'I appoint myself general. Let us hold a council of war! You, cuirassiers, are hereby ordered to cut off the enemy's retreat—that is to say, to lock the door. You, the grenadiers, shall act as my escort.'

"I executed the order; and then joined my forces with those of the main army, which was occupied in making a reconnaissance.

"Just as I had reached the rear of the main army behind a big screen, a furious noise burst upon my ears. I rushed forward with a candle in my hand. Le Poittevin had just thrust his bayonet through the chest of a mannikin; and

Sorieul was splitting the same mannikin's head with his ax. The error being discovered, the general commanded: 'Be prudent!'—and the military operations continued.

"For at least twenty minutes we rummaged every nook and corner of the studio without finding anything; when it occurred to Le Poittevin to open an immense cupboard which formed a recess in the wall. The recess was deep and dark. I advanced the light, and drew back in astonishment:—a man was there, looking at me, a real live man!

"Immediately I closed and double-locked the cupboard door; and a second council of war was decided upon.

"There was quite a difference of opinion. Sorieul proposed to smoke the robber out;—Le Poittevin proposed that he should be reduced by starvation;—I proposed to blow up the cupboard with gunpowder.

"But the advice of Le Poittevin prevailed; and, while he stood guard with his great gun, we went after what was left of the punch, and got our pipes. Then we sat down before the locked door, and drank a toast to the prisoner.

"After we had besieged the cupboard for about half-an-hour, Sorieul said:—'I want to get a good look at him, any-how. Suppose we take him by storm!'

"I shouted—'Bravo!'—each man clutched his weapons; the door of the cupboard was flung open; and Sorieul, cocking his unloaded pistol, charged in first.

"We followed him whooping. There was a frightful jostling in the darkness; and after five minutes of an awful struggle, we pulled out into the light a sort of very old bandit with white hair,—very ragged and very filthy.

"We tied him hand and foot, and placed him upon a chair. He did not utter a single word.

"Then Sorieul, permeated with the solemnity of drunkenness, turned toward us, saying:

" 'Now we shall proceed to judge this villain!'

"I was so drunk that this proposition appeared to me quite natural.

"Le Poittevin was ordered to act as counsel for the defense, and I to conduct the prosecution.

"The prisoner was condemned to death unanimously,—excepting the vote of the counsel for the defense.

" 'Let the sentence be at once executed,' said Sorieul. But a scruple arose in his mind. 'This man,' he exclaimed, 'ought not to die without being allowed to receive the consolations of religion. Suppose somebody goes for a priest.'

"I objected that it was too late in the night. Then Sorieul proposed that I should act as confessor; and he exhorted the criminal to confess himself to me.

"For five minutes the man's eyes had been rolling wildly;—he was doubtless asking himself in his terror what kind of people he was among. Then, in a cavernous, whiskey-burnt voice, he gasped out:—'You must be joking,—ain't you?' But Sorieul forced him to his knees; and observing that he feared the man's parents might have neglected to have had him baptized, he emptied over his skull a tumblerful of rum.

"Then he said to him:

" 'Confess yourself to this gentleman here!—your last hour has come.'

"In desperate terror the old rascal began to roar out *'Help! help!'* with such force, that we had to gag him at once to prevent him from rousing all the neighbours. Then he rolled upon the floor, writhing, kicking,—upsetting the furniture, bursting the canvasses. At last, Sorieul, getting out of patience, shouted: "Here! let us make an end of him right now!'

"And taking deliberate aim at the old wretch, as he lay upon the floor, he pulled the trigger of his pistol. The hammer fell with a dry click. Impelled by this example, I fired in my turn. My musket, which was an old flint-lock, sent out a flash that surprised me.

"Then Le Poittevin gravely uttered this observation:

" 'Are you sure we have the right to kill this man?'

"Sorieul, utterly astounded, replied:

" 'Haven't we condemned him to death?'

"But Le Poittevin went on:

" 'We cannot shoot civilians. This one should be delivered to the public executioner. We must take him to the police station.'

"The argument seemed to us quite conclusive. We picked the man up, and as he could not walk, we strapped him tightly to the plank of a model's-table; and I and Poittevin carried him down-stairs,—while Sorieul, armed to the teeth, brought up the rear.

"The sentinel at the station stopped us at the entrance. The *Chef-de-poste*, being summoned, recognized us at once; and as he had been a daily witness of our practical jokes, our tricks, our astounding inventions, he simply laughed and refused to take the prisoner.

"Sorieul insisted:—then the officer became angry, and ordered us in a tone that admitted of no reply, to take ourselves back home,—and that very quietly, too!

"The band therefore retraced its steps, and re-entered the studio. I asked:—'What are we to do with the robber?'

"Le Poittevin, feeling compassionate, observed that the man must feel very tired. And indeed he looked like a man in the last agonies of death, as he lay there tied to the plank,—all gagged and bound.

"Then I also became seized with pity,—the pity of a drunken man, and removing the gag, I asked him:

" 'Well, how do you like this sort of thing, my poor old chap?'

"He groaned out:

" 'I've had enough of it,—doggone the luck!'—(*or stronger words to the same effect.—T.*)

"Then Sorieul became absolutely paternal. He delivered the prisoner from all his bonds, made him take a chair, talked 'thee-and-thou' to him, and we all set to work to manufacture another punch in order to cheer him up. The robber sat very quietly in his arm-chair, and watched us. When the punch was ready we offered him a tumbler of it (we would have held his head if it had been necessary), and we all touched glasses before drinking.

"The prisoner drank like a regiment. But as the day began to dawn, he rose up, and observed in a very calm way:

" 'I've got to leave you all now, because, you see, I must go home.'

"We were overwhelmed with grief at his departure;—we did all we could to keep him a little longer, but he wouldn't stay.

"Then we all shook hands with him; and Sorieul went to the head of the stairs with a light to show him the way down, and shouted out to him:—'Look out for the step before the hall-door.' "

*   *   *   *   *   *   *

Everybody laughed who had listened to the story-teller. He got up, lit his pipe, and taking a position in front of us again, added:

"But the funniest thing about this story is that every word of it is true."

THE BAPTISM

THE BAPTISM

"COME, doctor, let us take a little cognac."

"With pleasure."

And the old naval physician, holding out his little glass, watched the beautiful golden-flashing liquid rise to its edges.

Then he lifted it on a level with his eye, so as to let the lamplight filter through it; he smelled it; sipped a few drops which he rolled about for a long time over his tongue and against the moist and sensitive flesh of his palate;—then he exclaimed.

"Oh! the charming poison!—the seductive murderer!—the delicious destroyer of nations!

"You do not know him—you! You have read, no doubt, that admirable book *L'Assommoir;* but you have never seen alcohol, as I have seen it, exterminate a whole tribe of savages, a little negro kingdom,—alcohol brought in kegs, and disembarked by red-bearded English sailors, in the most placid fashion imaginable.

"But—come to think of it,—I have seen, seen with my own eyes, a very queer and very impressive alcoholic drama,— and that quite near us, in Brittany, in a little village not far from Pont l'Abbé.

"I was living at that time, during a year's leave of absence, in a little country-house my father had left me. You know that low flat coast, where the wind whistles through the furze night and day,—where one sees here and there, lying down or standing up, those enormous stones which were once gods, and which have retained something weird in their posture, their deportment, their shape. It always seemed to me as if they were going to become animated, and that I could see them trooping away into the country, walking off with slow and ponderous steps, the steps of a granite colossus, —or even soaring on prodigious wings, wings of stone, up to the heaven of the Druids.

"The sea shuts in and dominates the horizon—a restless sea, full of black-headed rocks, always covered with a slime of foam, like rabid dogs on the watch for the fishermen.

"And they, the men, go out upon that sea which overturns their boats with one heave of its green back, and swallows them like pills. Day and night they go out in their little boats,—audacious, anxious, and drunk. They are very often drunk. 'When the bottle is full,' they say, 'one can see the rock; but when it is empty, the rock cannot be seen any more.'

"Go into one of their cabins! You will never find the father at home. And if you ask the wife where her husband is, she will point out to the gloomy sea which growls and spits out its white saliva all over the shore. He stayed in it one evening after he had drunk too much. And the oldest son stayed with him. She has still four boys,—four big fair haired strong boys. It will soon be their turn.

"Well, I was living at the time I speak of in a country-house near Pont l'Abbé. I lived there with one servant,—an old sailor,—a Breton family to whose care the property was entrusted during my absence. It consisted of three persons, —two sisters, and a man who had married one of them, and who used to take care of my garden.

"Now about Christmas, that year, my gardener's wife gave birth to a son.

"The husband came to ask me to stand godfather. I could not very well refuse; and he borrowed ten francs—for church expenses, he said.

"The ceremony was fixed for January 2d. For eight days the ground had been covered with snow,—an immense livid and solid carpet of snow that seemed to extend without limit over the whole low flat country. Far off behind the white plains, the sea looked perfectly black; and you could see it raging, hunching up its back and rolling its waves, as if it wanted to rush upon its pale neighbour, that seemed to be dead,—so cold and calm and sad it looked.

"At nine o'clock in the morning the father, Kérandec, came to my door with his sister-in-law,—Kermagan, a very tall girl, and the nurse, who carried the child wrapped up in a blanket.

"And we started for the church. It was terribly cold,—one

of those cold spells strong enough to split stones,—a frost that chapped the skin, and made one suffer horribly with the sensation of having been burned. As for me I kept thinking about the poor little creature that was being carried along before us; and I said to myself that this Breton race must be really made of iron, if the children could endure such promenades so soon after birth.

"We came to the church; but the door was still locked. The priest had not yet come.

"Then the nurse, sitting down upon a curb-stone near the threshold, began to strip the child. I thought at first there was something the matter; but then I saw that the child was being stripped naked—absolutely naked,—in the frozen air. I went up to the nurse, feeling quite angry at such an act of imprudence.

" 'Why, are you crazy!   Do you want to kill the child?'

" 'Oh, no, master—but the child must wait naked for the good God.' "

"The father and the aunt looked on with the greatest tranquillity. It was the custom of the country. It would bring bad luck to the child not to follow the custom.

"I got angry. I abused the man; I threatened to go back home; I tried to cover the frail creature by main force. But it was all in vain. The nurse ran away from me through the snow; and the body of the baby became violet.

"I was on the point of leaving these brutes, when I saw

the priest coming across the fields, followed by the sacristan and a little country boy.

"I ran to him, and expressed my indignation in violent language. He was not surprised,—did not quicken his pace, —did not hurry in the least. He simply replied:

" 'Why, sir, how can the thing be helped? It is the custom of the country. All the people follow it; and we cannot possibly prevent it.'

" 'But you can at least hurry up,' I replied.

"He replied:

" 'I am going just as fast as I can.'

"And he went in by the sacristy-door while we remained at the threshold, where I certainly suffered even more than the poor baby who kept screaming under the biting of the cold wind.

"At last the door was opened. We went in. But the child had to remain naked during the whole of the ceremony.

"It was interminably long. The priest mumbled the Latin syllables, which fell from his lips all mispronounced. He moved slowly,—with the slowness of a sacred tortoise; and the white surplice he wore chilled my heart, as if it were another sort of snow in which he had wrapped himself in order to make suffer still more, in the name of an inclement and barbarous God, that poor human larva who was being so tortured with cold.

"At last the baptism was finished according to all the rites; and I saw the nurse again wrap up the frozen baby in the blanket. It moaned with a piercing and plaintive moan.

"The priest said to me:

" 'Will you now come and sign the register?'

"I turned to my gardener and said to him: 'Go back home now as quick as you can; and warm that child at once.' And I gave him some advice what to do to prevent the child from getting a congestion of the lungs, if it had not got one already.

"The man promised to do as I advised; and he went off, together with his sister-in-law and the nurse. I followed the priest into the sacristy.

"When I had signed the document, he charged me five francs for expenses.

"As I had already given ten francs to the father, I refused to pay again. The priest threatened to tear out the leaf and annul the ceremony. I threatened to appeal to the Procureur de la Republique.

"The quarre' was a long one. I had to pay in the end.

"Immediately on getting back home, I tried to find out whether anything terrible had taken place. I ran to Kerandec's; but the father, the sister-in-law, and the nurse had not yet returned.

"The mother, left all alone, was shivering with cold there in her bed; and she was hungry, not having had anything to eat since the evening before.

" 'Where the devil did they go to?' I asked. She replied

without surprise or vexation. 'They're drinking to celebrate the event.' It was the custom. Then I thought about my ten francs disbursed for the payment of church-expenses, but which were being spent, no doubt, for the purchase of alcohol.

"I sent some soup to the mother and I ordered a good fire to be made in her room. I was anxious and furious—fully determined to give all those brutes notice to quit; and I kept asking myself in terror what was going to become of that miserable child.

"At six o'clock in the evening they had not yet returned.

"I ordered my servant to wait for them; and I went to bed.

"At daybreak I was awakened by my servant, who came in with the warm water for my morning shave.

" 'And Kerandec?' I asked, just as soon as I could get my eyes open.

"The man hesitated a moment—then stammered out:— 'Oh! sir, he came in after midnight, so drunk he couldn't walk, and the big girl Kermagan, too, and the nurse also. I think they must all have been sleeping in some ditch,—so that the child must have died without any of them knowing it.'

"I jumped right out of bed, crying out:

" 'What! the child is dead!'

" 'Yes, sir. They brought it to Kerandec, the mother. When she found out how it was she began to cry; so they made her drink to console her.'

" 'Made her drink!—how?'

" 'Yes, sir; but I didn't know about that until this morning. As Kerandec himself had no more brandy and no money,
he took the spirits out of the lamp you gave him; and the
whole four of them drank that as long as any of it was left.
The mother even drank so much it made her very sick.'

"I threw on my clothes in a hurry and rushed over to my
gardener's place,—with my cane in my hand, intending to
bang all these human beasts as soon as I could find them.

"The mother, drunk with the mineral essence, was lying
in agony beside the purple corpse of the child.

"Kerandec, the nurse, and the big Kermagan girl, were
all snoring on the ground.

"I had to give immediate attention to the mother; but she
died about midday."

*   *   *   *   *   *   *

The old doctor ceased to speak. He again took up the
cognac bottle, poured himself out another drink; and once
more holding the blond liquor up against the lamplight which
seemed to fill his glass with the very essence of molten topaz,
he swallowed the perfidious and fiery fluid at a gulp.

ON HORSEBACK

ON HORSEBACK

. . . Hector de Gribelin had been brought up in the
country, in the paternal home,—under the care of an old
priest, who was his tutor. The family was not rich; but
was able to keep up appearances very well.

Then when he was twenty, they tried to find a situation
for him; and he managed to get into the Marine Office
on a salary of 1,500 francs a year. He found himself ship-
wrecked upon that shoal, like all who are not prepared at
an early age for the rough battle of life,—all who see existence through a cloud, who ignore means and ways of resistance,—all in whom special aptitudes, particular faculties,
a keen energy for struggle, have not been cultivated in early
childhood,—all who have been sent out into the world without weapons or tools in their hands.

His first three years of office-life were horrible.

He had managed to find some family friends—old-fashioned people of small means,—who lived in the aristocratic
and dismal streets of the Faubourg Saint-Germain;—and he
had made for himself a little circle of acquaintances.

Humble, yet proud, and totally ignorant of modern life,
these needy aristocrats occupied the upper floors of sleepy-
looking houses. From garret to cellar, every tenant in these

houses had a title; but money seemed to be as scarce on the first floor as in the sixth story.

Everlasting prejudices, the preoccupation of rank, the terror of falling from position, haunted all these once brilliant families, ruined by inactivity. In this society Hector de Gribelin met a young girl as noble and poor as himself, and married her.

They had four children in two years.

*   *   *   *   *   *   *

During four years more the household, harassed by poverty, knew of no better amusements than Sunday walks in the Champs-Elysées, and some visits to the theatre—once or twice every winter,—thanks to free tickets procured by a fellow-clerk.

But, all unexpectedly, about the commencement of spring, some extra work was confided to the employé by his superintendent; and an extra remuneration of 300 francs was accorded to him.

He said to his wife when he brought the money home:

"My dear Henriette, we must really give ourselves some little enjoyment—say a pleasure party for the children."

And after a long discussion it was resolved to have a picnic in the country.

"*Ma foi!*" cried Hector, "once does not mean a habit; we can hire an open carriage for you, the children, and the nurse, and I'll hire a horse at the livery-stable. It will do me good."

And during the whole week, they talked of nothing but the excursion.

Every evening, when he came home from the office, Hector would take his oldest boy, make him straddle his leg, and jump him up and down, saying:

"This is the way papa's going to ride, next Sunday, on the promenade."

And all the rest of the day the little fellow was straddling chairs and dragging them all around the hall:

"This is papa, on his horse."

And the old servant herself began to look at her master with wondering respect, at the mere idea that he was going to accompany the carriage on horseback; and during every meal, she heard him talking about the art of riding, or telling about his exploits of other days, on his father's place. Oh! he had been trained in a good school; and once he found himself on an animal's back, he was afraid of nothing— nothing in the world!

He kept repeating to his wife, rubbing his hands together the while:

"If they would only give me an animal a little hard to manage, I would be delighted. You'll see how I can ride; and, if you wish, we'll come back by way of the Champs-Elysées as the people are returning from the Bois de Boulogne. We're going to make quite a nice show; and I wouldn't mind meeting someone from the Marine Office. Nothing like these little things to make a man stand well with the superintendent."

On the appointed day, horse and carriage were simultaneously at the door. He went out and looked at the animal. He had had foot straps attached to his pantaloons the day before; and had been playing with a new riding-whip since the previous evening.

He lifted up and felt each of the horse's legs, one after another; patted his neck, his ribs, his flanks, tested his back with his finger; opened his mouth, declared his age; and, as the rest of the family came out, he gave a sort of little lecture, theoretical and practical, about horses in general, and that horse in particular, which he declared to be excellent.

When all had taken their respective places in the carriage, he looked to the saddle-girths, and then, climbing on a stirrup, fell on the back of the animal, which began to dance under the burden, and very nearly threw its rider.

Hector, feeling a little uneasy, tried to quiet him.

"Come, that's all right, my friend,—that's all right."

Then when the horse had resumed his tranquillity, and the rider his self-possession, the latter asked:

"Well, are you all ready?"

All the voices answered at once:

"Yes."

Then he gave the word of command.—"Go ahead!"

And the cavalcade started.

All eyes were turned upon him. He trotted in the English

style,—with exaggerations of the motion. Every time he fell down upon the saddle he went up again, as if being shot into space. Very often he seemed on the point of falling over the horse's mane; and he looked straight before him,— his face very pinched and his cheeks very pale.

His wife, holding one of her children on her lap, and the nurse, who held another, kept saying all the time:

"Look at papa!—look at papa!"

And the two little ones, delighted with the motion, the joy, and the bright air, uttered shrill cries. Frightened by these clamours, the horse broke into a gallop; and while the rider tried to check him his hat flew off and rolled on the ground. Then the driver had to get down and pick it up; and as Hector received it he shouted out to his wife from a distance:

"Try to keep the children from screaming like that; you'll have the horse running away with me!"

*   *   *   *   *   *   *

They breakfasted on the grass, in the Bois du Vesinet, with the provisions they had brought along in a box.

Although the carriage-driver looked after the three horses, Hector was always getting up to see if his own animal did not want something or other; and he patted him on the neck —made him eat bread, and cakes, and sugar.

He declared:

"He is a first-rate trotter. He even shook me up a little at first; but you saw how quickly I got over it;—he found he had his master, and now he won't try to play any more tricks."

As he had decided, the party returned by way of the Champs-Elysées.

The vast avenue swarmed with carriages. And the pedestrians, on either side, were so numerous that it seemed as if two huge black ribbons were being unrolled from the Arc de Triomphe to the Place de la Concorde. A deluge of sunlight fell over it all; flashing on the varnish of vehicles, the polished steel of harnesses, the handles of carriage-doors.

A madness of movement, an intoxication of life, seemed to agitate all that crowd of people, carriages, and animals. And far off, the Obelisk towered in a mist of gold.

No sooner had Hector's horse passed the Arc de Triomphe, than he was seized with a new ardour; and he shot forward at full trot towards the stable, despite all the efforts of his rider to rein him in.

The carriage was far behind now,—very far; and right in front of the Palais de l'Industrie, the horse, finding the way clear, turned to the right and broke into a gallop.

An old woman in an apron was crossing the street, very quietly; she happened to be just in Hector's way, as he came along at full speed. Powerless to master his beast, he yelled with all his might:

"Hello there!—hey!—look out!—hey!"

She might have been deaf, for she kept peacefully proceeding on her way until the exact moment when, stricken by the chest of the horse rushing forward like a locomotive, she went rolling ten yards off, with her petticoats in the air, after having turned three somersaults upon her head.

Voices shouted:

"Stop him!—stop him!"

Hector hung on to the horse's mane, yelling:

"Help!"

A terrible shock suddenly sent him flying like a ball over the ears of the trotter, to fall right into the arms of a police sergeant who had rushed in front of him.

In another second, a furious and gesticulating crowd had gathered about him. And a certain old gentleman, who had a big round decoration on his breast, and wore a big white moustache, seemed particularly exasperated. He repeated over and over again:

"*Sacrebleu!* when a man's as clumsy as you, he ought to stay at home. When a man doesn't know how to ride a horse, he mustn't go out into the street to kill people."

But then four men appeared, carrying the old woman. She looked as if dead, with her cap all awry over her yellow face,—and all grey with dust.

"Take that woman to the nearest drugstore," ordered the old gentleman; "and then let us go to the police station."

Hector walked along, between two policemen. A third led his horse. A crowd followed them; and all of a sudden the hired carriage made its appearance. His wife leaped out; the nurse seemed to lose her wits; the children whimpered. He explained that he would be home soon, that he had accidentally knocked a woman down,—that the whole affair amounted to nothing. And his family went off, wild with grief.

At the police station matters were very quickly explained. He had to give his name,—Hector de Gribelin, clerk at the Marine Office; and was held to await news about the injured woman. A police officer was sent to make inquiries, and soon returned. He said that she had returned to consciousness, but was complaining about awful pains in her inside. She was a housekeeper, sixty-five years of age; and was known as Madame Simon.

When he found she was not dead, Hector breathed freely, and promised to pay the expenses of her cure. Then he rushed to the drugstore.

There was a mob in front of the door. The old woman, sitting in a chair, was moaning and groaning with her arms pending inert on either side, and an expression of stupor upon her face. Two doctors were still examining her. No bones were broken; but they were afraid of internal lesions.

Hector asked her:

"Are you suffering much pain?"

"Oh! yes!"

"Where is it hurting you?"

"It's like I had a fire in my stomach."

A doctor approached and asked:

"You are the gentleman who caused the accident?"

"Yes, sir."

"Well, this woman must be sent to an hospital; I know a place where they will take her for six francs a day. Would you like me to have her taken there?"

Hector thanked him delightedly, and went home comforted.

His wife was waiting for him in tears. He soothed her.

"It doesn't amount to anything. This woman Simon is already much better; in three days more she'll be all right again. I had her sent to an hospital;—it won't amount to anything. . . . It won't amount to anything at all."

As soon as he left the office next day he went to see after Madame Simon. He found her swallowing a big bowlful of soup, in a very contented manner.

"Well!" he asked.

She answered:

"Oh! my poor dear gentleman; it's just the same thing. I feel as if there was nothing left of me. I ain't a bit better."

The doctor declared it would be necessary to await developments—he was afraid of complications.

Hector waited three days;—then he went back again. The old woman's skin looked healthy; her eye was bright and clear; but the moment she saw him, she began to whine:

"I can't so much as move myself, my poor dear gentleman! —I can't move myself at all. I have got something's going to last me till the end of my days."

Hector felt a cold shiver run down his back. He asked the doctor what he thought about it. The doctor lifted up his hands:

"What can I do about it, my dear sir?—I can't tell! She screams when any effort is made to lift her up. Even her chair can't be moved from one place to another without causing her to scream horribly. I must believe what she tells me, sir;—I can't see inside of her. So long as I don't actually see her walk, I have no right to think she is lying."

The old woman listened without moving,—watched with her cunning eyes.

Eight days passed, then fifteen, then a whole month, Madame Simon never left her chair. She ate from morning until night, got fat, chatted merrily with the other patients; and she seemed to have become quite accustomed to immobility— as if it were a reward of rest well-earned by fifty years' of going up and down staircases, turning mattresses, carrying coal from floor to floor, sweeping and dusting.

Hector came every day to see her, terrified as he was by this new situation; he always found her cool and calm, and always declaring:

"I can't move myself a bit, my poor dear gentleman;— can't move myself a bit."

Every evening Madame Gribelin, devoured with an anguish, would ask:

"And Madame Simon?"

And every time he would answer her in a tone of discouragement and despair:

"No difference!—just the same thing."

Then Hector appealed to four celebrated physicians, who gathered around the old woman. She let them examine her, feel her—watching them all the time with her sly old eyes.

"Got to make her walk," said one.

She screamed out:

"I can't, my good gentlemen—I can't; I can't."

Then they seized, and pulled her out of the chair, and dragged her along a few steps; but she slipped from their hands and crumbled down all of a heap on the floor, uttering such hideous cries that they carried her back to the chair again, with infinite precaution.

The four physicians gave a discreet opinion—nevertheless concluding that the old woman could not possibly do any more work.

And when Hector carried the news home to his wife, she let herself fall into a chair, exclaiming:

"It would be infinitely better to bring her here; it would cost us far less."

He leaped up at the mere idea:

"Here?—here with us!—how can you think of such a thing?"

But she, resigned by this time to anything and everything, only responded with tears in her eyes:

"What else is to be done, my dear?—it is not my fault!"

THE OLD CRIPPLE

THE OLD CRIPPLE

HE had known better days, notwithstanding his appearance of misery and infirmity.

At the age of fifteen, he had had both legs crushed by a vehicle passing on the Varville highway. Since that time he had begged along the roads, from one farmyard to another, balancing himself upon his crutches, the constant use of which had pushed up his shoulders to a level with his ears. His head seemed as if buried between two hills.

Found in a ditch by the parish priest of Billettes on the eve of All Saints, and for that reason christened with the name of Nicholas Toussaint;—brought up by charity, and without a particle of education;—crippled for life after having been persuaded to take a few drinks of brandy—just for a joke!—by the village baker; and ever since that time a tramp,—the only thing he knew in the world was how to hold out his hand.

In other years the Baroness d'Avary used to allow him to sleep in a sort of kennel, full of straw, close to the hen-house, in the farm attached to the Château; and when desperately hungry, he was always sure of being able to get a piece of bread and a glass of cider in the kitchen. Sometimes he used also to get a few coppers thrown down to him by the old lady from the top of her terrace-steps, or from the windows of her room. Now she was dead.

In the villages they would give him scarcely anything; he was too well known; people had become tired of the sight of him;—they had seen him for forty long years going from farmhouse to farmhouse, pulling his ragged and deformed body along, with the aid of his two wooden legs. Still he did not want to go away, because all of the world he knew anything about was that one little patch of country, with its three or four villages, through which he had been dragging his miserable existence. He had laid down a frontier line for his beggary; and he could never have gone beyond the limits which he had never accustomed himself to cross.

He did not know whether the world extended very far beyond the line of trees which had always been the boundary of his vision. He did not even ask himself whether it did or did not. And when the peasants, weary of seeing him always hobbling along their fields or sitting down beside their ditches, would shout out to him,—"Why don't you go to the other villages instead of always crutching about here?"—he would never make a reply, but simply take himself off, full of a vague fear of the unknown,—the fear of a poor creature who dreads a thousand different things in a sort of confused way, —new faces, abuse, the suspicious observation of people who did not know him, and the gendarmes who walked the road two by two, and the very sight of whom made him instinctively slink behind bushes or stone-heaps.

Whenever he saw them coming in the distance, glittering in their uniforms under the sunlight, he would suddenly develop an extraordinary agility—the agility of a monster,—in seeking a hiding-place. He would tumble down from his crutches,—letting himself fall flat like a rag; and then he would roll himself all up into a ball, become quite little, become invisible, lie flat like a hare in its lair, so as to make his brown rags seem a part of the ground that they resembled in colour.

Nothwithstanding, he had never had any trouble with them in his life. But he had the instinctive fear of them in his blood, as though he had inherited the fear and cunning of those parents whom he had never known.

He had no refuge, no roof, no hut, no shelter. He slept anywhere in summer; and in winter he slipped under barns or into stables with astonishing address. He always got away in the morning before any one had suspected his presence. He knew all the holes through which he could get into the farm-buildings; and as the constant use of crutches had given him extraordinary power in his arms, he was able to climb hand over hand into the haylofts, where he would often remain three or four days at a time without moving,—especially when he had been able to collect some provisions upon his rounds.

He lived like the beasts of the fields, in the midst of men, without knowing anybody, without loving anybody;—the feeling toward him among the peasants was simply one of in-

different contempt and resigned hostility. They had nicknamed him Cloche (*the bell*) because he swung along between his crutches like a bell between its supports.

For two whole days he had eaten nothing at all. Nobody
would give him a bit more. People had finally got tired of
him. The peasant-women, at their doors, would scream out
to him from a distance when they saw him coming.

"Get away from here, you old clodhopper! Didn't I give
you a piece of bread only three days ago?"

Then he would pivot round upon his crutches and take
himself to the neighbouring house, only to be there received
in like manner.

From door to door the women cried out:

"One can't undertake to feed that loafer all the year round,
anyhow!"

Nevertheless the loafer had to get something to eat every
day.

He had gone all through Saint-Hilaire, Varville, and Les
Billettes, without being able to get one copper or one hard
crust of bread. There was no hope for him consequently except at Tournolles; but he had to travel two leagues on the
public highway to get there; and he felt already so weak
that he could hardly drag himself along, having his stomach
as empty as his pocket.

Nevertheless he started.

It was December; a cold wind played over the fields, and
whistled through the naked branches; while the clouds were

rushing through a low-hanging dark sky, as if hurrying God knows where.

The cripple moved on slowly, lifting up his crutches with a painful effort, and relying also a little upon the extremity of the one leg left him, terminated by a clubfoot and clad with a rag.

From time to time he would sit down on the edge of the roadside ditch, and rest himself a little. Hunger had created a strange distress in his dull and vague mind. He had but one definite idea—"to eat"; but how to get anything to eat he did not know.

For three whole hours he worried slowly along the road;— then, when at last he caught sight of the village-trees, he quickened his movements.

The first peasant he met and asked alms of, answered him:

"You here again, you old fraud! Seems that I'm never going to be rid of you!"

And Cloche went off. At every door he was roughly received, and turned away without being given anything. Patient and persistent, he nevertheless continued his round. He could not collect one cent.

Then he visited the farms, shambling over the rain-soaked clay of the fields,—so extenuated that he could not lift his crutches properly. He was driven from every gate. It was one of those cold and dismal days when hearts are contracted, when minds are irritable, when the disposition is gloomy, when no hand is voluntarily extended either to give or to help.

When he had visited all the houses he knew, he let himself fall his whole length at the edge of a ditch beside the farmyard of Maitre Chiquet. He "unhung himself" as they used to say in order to describe the manner in which he let himself tumble down from between his high crutches by letting them slip up through his arms. And he lay there a long time motionless, tortured by hunger, but too much stupefied to really appreciate his fathomless misery.

He was waiting for something, he knew not what,—with that vague hope which constantly persists in each and all of us. He waited there, at the corner of that farmyard for that mysterious aid we are always expecting to receive either from heaven or from men, without asking how, or why, or by whom it is to come. A troop of black chickens came by, seeking their nourishment in that earth which nourishes all creatures. At every second, they pecked at a grain or some invisible insect, and continued their slow sure search.

Cloche looked at them without thinking of anything; then he got,—rather into his stomach than into his head,—the idea, or rather the sensation, that one of those things would be good to eat roasted over a brushwood fire.

No suspicion that he was about to commit a theft ever once occurred to him. He seized a stone within reach of his hand; and as he was a skilful thrower, he killed at once with his stone the nearest chicken.

The rest ran away, swaying on their thin legs; and Cloche, climbing up on his crutches, again began to hobble after his game, with motions precisely like those of the chickens.

But just as he came up to where the little black body lay, with its head all blood-stained, he received a terrible shove in the back which obliged him to let go his crutches, and which sent him rolling on his face ten yards away. And Maitre Chiquet, thoroughly exasperated, rushed on the marauder, beat him furiously, striking like a madman,—as a robbed peasant always strikes,—thumping with fist and knees all the body of the cripple, who was utterly powerless to defend himself.

The field hands ran up, and took a turn in helping the master to beat the beggar. Then, when they had all beaten and kicked him until they were tired, they lifted him up and carried him to the woodhouse, and locked him up there; and sent for the police.

Cloche, bleeding and half dead with hunger, remained upon the ground. Evening came, then night, then morning. All this time he had not had anything to eat.

About noon, the police came, and opened the door of the woodhouse with all possible precaution; for they expected resistance, as Maitre Chiquet had told them the beggar had made a violent attack upon him, and that he had only been able to defend himself with extreme difficulty.

One of the gendarmes cried out:

"Here, you!—get up out of that!"

But Cloche could not move himself. He tried to hoist his body once more on the stilts and failed. They thought it was all a feint, a trick, one of the regular dodges practiced by thieves; and the two armed men, seizing him violently, lifted him upon his crutches by main force.

His old fear had come upon him—the hereditary fear of the policeman's yellow sword-belt,—like the fear of the game in the presence of the hunter, the natural fear of the mouse before the cat. And by a superhuman effort he managed to remain erect.

"March!" shouted the officer. And he hobbled along. All the farm people assembled to watch him going. The women shook their fists at him; the men jeered and swore at him. He was caught at last anyhow. Good riddance!

And he passed away, between his two captors. He found desperate energy enough to keep so dragging himself along until evening,—being too stupefied even to know what had happened to him,—too terrified to understand anything.

People passing on the road stopped to look at him go by; and the peasants muttered:

"Must be some robber."

Toward night they arrived at the *chef-lieu* of the canton. He had never been that far before. He really had no idea what had happened, nor what was going to happen. All these terrible and unexpected things, new houses, strange faces, absolutely terrified him out of his wits.

He never uttered a single word,—having nothing, indeed,

to say; for he had ceased to be able to understand anything. Besides, during all the years that he had never talked with any one, he had gradually lost the use of his tongue through want of habit; and whatever thoughts he had left would have been of too confused a sort to be expressed in words.

He was locked up in the village jail. It never occurred to the policemen that he might need something to eat; and they left him there until next day.

But they found him lying dead on the floor, when they went to question him, early in the morning. How surprised they were!

DENIS

DENIS

Monsieur Marambot opened the letter his servant Denis brought him, and smiled.

Denis, who had been in his employ for twenty years,—a little jolly thickset man, who was constantly referred to, through all the country round, as the very model of a valet,—queried:

"Monsieur is happy?—Monsieur has received some good news?"

Monsieur Marambot was not rich. He was a bachelor, and had been a village druggist for many years. He now lived quietly on the small revenue made with great difficulty by selling medicines to the country people. He answered:

"Yes, my boy. Old Malois does not want to go into court; and to-morrow I will get my money. Five thousand francs will help an old bachelor along pretty well."

And M. Marambot rubbed his hands together. He was a man of a rather resigned character, not particularly jovial,—incapable of anything like sustained effort, and quite indifferent about his own affairs.

He might easily have made a better living by taking advantage of the death of certain fellow-druggists, who had stores well-situated in large centres, to take one of the vacant businesses and so assure himself of a lucrative custom. But the trouble of moving, and the thought of all the other things he would have to do, always prevented it; and after thinking over the matter for a day or two, he would merely say:

"Ah! bah!—next time I'll really think about it. One loses nothing by waiting, anyhow. Perhaps I'll get a still better chance."

Denis, on the contrary, was always urging his master to attempt something. Naturally energetic, he would declare:

"Oh! as for me, if I just had the capital to start with, I would have made a fortune. Only a thousand francs, and I'd make my way soon enough."

M. Marambot smiled without replying, went out into his little garden, and walked up and down with his hands behind him, in a revery.

Denis, all day long, sang ballads and country songs, as if he were in an uncommonly good humour. He even showed unusual activity; for he cleaned all the window-panes in the house, singing at the top of his voice while he wiped the glass.

Astonished at his zeal, M. Marambot said to him several times, with a smile:

"If you keep on working like that, my boy, you will have nothing to do to-morrow."

Next morning, about 9 o'clock, the postman handed Denis four letters for his master, one of which was very heavy.

M. Marambot at once locked himself up in his room, and remained there until late in the afternoon. He then entrusted his servant with four letters for the post. One of them was addressed to M. Malois;—it was no doubt an acknowledgment of money received.

Denis asked his master no questions; he seemed to be that day as melancholy and sullen as he had been merry the evening before.

Night came. M. Marambot went to bed at his usual hour, and slept.

He was awakened by a singular noise. He sat up at once in his bed and listened. But all at once his bedroom door opened, and Denis appeared on the scene,—holding a candle in one hand and a kitchen-knife in the other! his eyes wild and fixed; his lips compressed as if under the influence of some terrible emotion, and his face so pale that he looked like a ghost.

Monsieur Marambot, at first stricken dumb with astonishment, concluded that Denis was walking in his sleep, and he got up to intercept him, when Denis suddenly blew out the light and made a rush for the bed. His master instinctively put out his hands to save himself from the shock of the encounter, which flung him upon his back; and then he tried to seize the hands of the domestic, who seemed to have become demented, and who was striking at him with all his might.

The first blow of the knife struck him in the shoulder;

the second blow he received in his forehead, the third in his chest. He struggled frantically, putting out his hands in the dark, and kicking out with his feet, shouting:

"Denis! Denis!—are you mad?—Denis! What are you doing?—Denis!"

But Denis, panting with his efforts, still kept striking, became more and more furious;—sometimes a kick or a blow would fling him back, but he always rushed on again, wildly. Monsieur Marambot received two more wounds,—one in the leg and one in the abdomen. But a sudden thought came to him, and he screamed out:

"Stop, Denis!—stop!—I have not yet got my money!"

The man at once stopped striking. Monsieur Marambot could hear him panting in the dark.

M. Marambot spoke again:

"I have not yet got a cent. M. Malois has gone back on his word; the case is going before the courts;—that is why you took those letters to the post. You had better read the letters lying on my desk."

And with a supreme effort, he managed to get hold of the matches on the table, and to strike a light.

He was covered with blood. Jets of it had spattered the wall. The sheets, the bed-curtains,—everything was red. Denis, also bloody from head to foot, was standing in the middle of the room.

When he saw all this, Monsieur Marambot thought it was all over with him, and became unconscious.

He came to himself again at daylight. It took him some little time to collect his senses,—to understand,—to remember. But suddenly the recollection of the attempt, and the sensation of his wounds came to him; and so intense a fear took possession of him that he shut his eyes so as not to see anything. At the end of a few minutes, his terror calmed; and he began to think. He had not died from the blows,—therefore he had some chance of living. He felt weak—very weak, but had no violent pain, though he felt a soreness at various points of his body, as of severe pinching. He also felt very chill, and wet, and compressed, as if he had been tightly swathed with bandages. He thought the humidity must be blood; and a shudder passed through him at the thought of all that red fluid which had issued from his own veins in such quantity as to wet his bed. The idea of having to see that awful sight again completely upset him; and he shut his eyes as tightly as he could, as if afraid they might open in spite of him.

What had become of Denis? He must have run away.

But what was he, Marambot, now going to do? To get up, and call for help? Why, if he were to make the least movement, all his wounds would certainly break open again, and he would die from loss of blood.

All of a sudden, he heard his bedroom door pushed open. His heart almost stopped. That was certainly Denis coming back to finish him. He tried to hold his breath so that the murderer would think he was really dead,—that the job was thoroughly done.

He felt the sheet pulled off,—then felt some one feeling his abdomen. A sharp pain near his hip made him start. Now he felt somebody washing his wound,—very gently,— with cold water. Therefore the crime must have been dis- covered; and they were attending to his wounds;—he was being nursed. A wild joy came on him; but through a lingering sense of prudence, he tried not to show that he was conscious,—and he half opened one eye, only one, with ever so many precautions.

He recognized Denis standing beside him,—Denis himself! Good Lord! He shut his eyes again forthwith.

Denis! What on earth was he doing? What did he want? What frightful project was he now endeavouring to accom- plish?

What was he doing? Why, he was washing him simply to hide all traces of the crime. And now, perhaps, he would bury him, ten feet deep, in the garden, so that nobody could ever find him. Or else, perhaps, in the cellar,—under the place where the bottles of choice wine were kept.

And M. Marambot began to tremble so much that every limb shook.

He thought: "It is all up with me,—all up with me!" He shut his eyes not to see the last blow of the knife coming. It did not come. Denis was now lifting him, and binding his wounds with some linen. Then he began to bind the wound in the leg, very carefully, as he had learned to do when his master was a druggist.

There could be no more doubt in the mind of anyone who knew the business. The servant, after having tried to kill him, was now trying to save him.

Then, in a dying voice, M. Marambot gave him this piece of practical counsel:

"The washing and dressing ought to be done with carbolic acid diluted with soap and water."

Denis answered—

"That's what I'm doing, Monsieur."

M. Marambot opened both his eyes.

There was no trace of blood now,—either in the bed, or on the wall, or in the room, or upon the person of the assassin. The wounded man was lying upon clean white sheets.

The two men looked at one another.

Finally, M. Marambot said very gently:

"You have committed a great crime."

Denis replied:

"I am trying to make reparation for it, Monsieur. If you promise not to denounce me, I will continue to serve you as faithfully as in the past."

Well, it was not just the most propitious time to argue with his servant. M. Marambot, as he closed his eyes again, articulated:

"I swear to you that I will never denounce you."

*   *   *   *   *   *   *

Denis saved his master. He passed whole nights and days without sleep,—never leaving the patient's room a moment,—preparing lotions, mixing medicines,—giving doses,—feeling his master's pulse, counting it anxiously,—managing the case with the skill of a professional nurse, and the devotion of a son.

Every minute or two he would ask:

"Well, Monsieur, how do you feel now?"

Monsieur Marambot would reply, feebly:

"A little better, my boy—thank you!"

And often, when the wounded man awoke in the night, he would see his nurse weeping silently as he sat in the arm-chair by the bed, and wiping his eyes.

Never in his life had the old druggist been so well cared for,—so much petted and caressed. At first he had said to himself:

"Just so soon as I get well, I'll get rid of this rascal."

But when he was fully convalescent, he kept putting off the man's dismissal from day to day. He thought to himself that no other person would ever show him so much attention, or bestow upon him so much care. He had a hold on the man now,—could control him by fear; and he even told him that he had made a will and deposited it with a notary, in which will was a statement denouncing Denis in case anything should occur.

This precaution seemed to assure him against any further attempt on his life; and then he began to ask himself whether it would not be better to keep the man anyhow, as he could thus keep a better watch over his future actions.

He found it was impossible to make up his mind about this matter, as he had found it formerly impossible to decide whether to open a drug store or not.

"Well, there's time enough to think about that," he would say to himself.

Meanwhile Denis continued to show himself to be a perfect domestic. M. Marambot got well. He kept Denis.

. . . But one morning just as he had finished breakfast, he suddenly heard a great noise in the kitchen. He ran thither, and saw Denis struggling in the grasp of two gendarmes.

One of the officers began to take notes in a notebook.

As soon as he saw his master, the servant sobbed out:

"You denounced me, Monsieur!—after all your promises! That is not right. You broke your word of honour, M. Marambot!—that was not right!—that was not right!"

Monsieur Marambot, utterly astounded, and greatly pained at being thus suspected, lifted up his hand, and said:

"I swear to you, before God, my boy, that I never denounced you. I have not even got the faintest idea how these policemen ever heard of the attempt to murder me!"

The one who was taking notes, gave a start:

"What!—you say he tried to murder you, M. Marambot?"

More and more confused, the druggist answered:

"Why, yes . . . but I never denounced him . . . I never

said a word about it . . . I swear I never said a word. . . .
He served me very well ever since."

The officer severely replied:

"I note down your statement. Justice will take full cog-
nizance of this new fact, which was not known to us before,
Monsieur Marambot. I was simply ordered to arrest your
servant for stealing two ducks from Monsieur Duhamel;—we
have witnesses to prove the theft. Sorry, Monsieur Marambot;—I shall testify to what you have just said."

Then turning to the gendarmes, he said:

"Take him along."

They took Denis along.

*   *   *   *   *   *   *

. . . The attorney for the defendant entered a plea of
insanity,—using the two different charges to make a case
for his client. He proved clearly that the theft of the two
ducks must have been performed in the same mental condition
which caused the eight knife-stabs to have been inflicted upon
M. Marambot. He made a very fine analysis of all the
different phases of this mental aberration, which, he felt
sure, he said, would yield to a few weeks' judicious medical
treatment in a good private asylum. He spoke enthusiastically
of the continuous self-devotion of his honest servant,—the
unceasing care he had bestowed upon the employer he had
wounded in a moment of mental aberration.

Monsieur Marambot, painfully impressed by the awful
recollection of that night, felt the tears rise to his eyes.

The shrewd lawyer noticed it,—spread out his arms with a great gesture, waved the long black sleeves of his robe like bats' wings, and vociferated in a sonorous tone:

"Look! look! look! gentlemen of the jury!—look at those tears! . . . What more need I now say in behalf of my client? What argument, what discourse, what reasoning could weigh against the evidence of those tears of his own master? Those tears plead louder than my voice;—they plead louder than the Voice of the Law;—they cry out for pardon for the madness of a moment! They implore; they absolve; they bless!" . . .

He held his peace, and sat down.

Turning to Marambot, whose testimony had been all in favor of Denis, the Judge asked:

"But in any event, sir,—even admitting that you believe this man to be insane,—I cannot understand your reason for keeping him in your employ. He was, under all circumstances, dangerous."

Marambot replied, wiping his eyes:

"What else could I do, your Honour?—it is so hard to find servants nowadays . . . I might have found worse."

Denis was acquitted and sent to an insane asylum, at his master's expense.

THE WOLF

THE WOLF

(Abbreviated from "Clair de Lune.")

. . . Monsieur D'Arville must have repeated the story often; for he related it fluently, never hesitating over words skilfully chosen for picturesque effect.

"Gentlemen," he said, "I never hunted in my life, nor my father. But my great-grandfather was the son of a man who hunted more than all of you put together. He died in 1764. I am going to tell you how.

"His name was Jean; he was married, father of the child destined to become my ancestor; and he lived with his younger brother, François d'Arville, in our old château in Lorraine, which was situated in the forest.

François d'Arville had remained a bachelor for pure love of hunting.

Both of them used to go hunting together; they hunted from one year's end to the other, without rest, without a pause, without ever getting tired. That was all they liked, all they understood, all they talked about, all they lived for.

It was a passion with both of them,—terrible, inexorable. It consumed them, filled their entire being, left no place for anything else.

They had given orders that they were never to be interrupted while hunting, under any pretext whatever. My ancestor was born while his father was chasing a fox, and Jean never thought of stopping his hunt on receiving the news: he only swore,—*"Nom d'un nom!*—the little rascal might very well have waited till after the death!"

His brother François was a still more furious hunter. As soon as he got up of a morning, he would go to look after the dogs and the horses;—then he would shoot birds around the château until time came to start on a chase for bigger game.

The country people used to call them The Marquis and the Junior. . . . Both were extraordinarily tall, bony, hairy, violent, and strong. The younger, who was still taller than his brother, had a voice so powerful, that according to a popular saying which he was proud to hear repeated, all the leaves of the forest trembled when he shouted.

And when they started off on horseback for the chase together, it must have been a fine sight to see the two giants bestraddling their great horses.

Now about the middle of the winter of 1764, the cold became excessive, and the wolves grew ferocious.

They would even attack peasants going home late; they prowled around the houses during the night, howled from sunset until sunrise, and depopulated the stables.

And after a time, a very ugly rumour began to spread. It was said that a colossal gray wolf, which had eaten two children, devoured a woman's arm, strangled all the watchdogs of the country,—showed no fear of entering enclosures and regularly went about at night, smelling under the doors. All the country people declared that they had felt his breath,—that it made the lights flicker. And a panic seized upon the whole province. No one dared venture out after dark. All the shadows seemed haunted by the image of the beast.

The D'Arville brothers resolved to find him and kill him, and they invited all the gentlemen of the country to a great hunt.

It was all in vain. They scoured all the forests, searched all the thickets without avail; they could never find him. They killed plenty of wolves, but not that particular wolf. And each night regularly, after the hunt, the animal would attack some belated traveller or devour some animal,—as if just to avenge himself,—and this always at quite a distance from where the last hunt had taken place.

At last one night he got into the pig-sties at the Château d'Arville, and devoured the two finest pigs.

The brothers become full of rage,—considering this attack as an open defiance on the monster's part. They got all their largest and best trained hounds together, and went to the chase in a great fury.

From earliest dawn until the red sun began to sink behind the naked trees, they scoured the thickets in vain.

At last, disappointed beyond measure, and angered in proportion, they began to ride homewards at a walk, along a road bordered with high bushes; wondering the while how all their science could have been baffled by this wolf,—feeling suddenly a sort of mysterious fear.

The elder said:

"That's no common animal. Seems he thinks like a man."

The younger replied:

"Perhaps we ought to get our cousin, the bishop, to bless a bullet for us, or get some priest to pronounce the necessary words."

They kept silence a while.

Jean spoke again:

"Look how red that sun is! The wolf is going to do some more mischief to-night."

He had scarcely spoken when his horse reared;—that of his brother François began to plunge. A great bush covered with dead leaves parted, and a huge animal—all gray—leaped out and shot through the woods.

Both men uttered something like a growl of joy, and bending over the necks of their powerful horses, they flung them forward with one immense effort of the whole body,—shot them on with such a vim,—exciting them with voice, gesture and spur,—that the strong riders actually seemed to be lifting the weighty steeds between their thighs, and flying away with them.

On they went at full speed, crashing through thickets, crossing ravines, scaling steeps, thundering down gorges, and blowing their horns with all the force of their lungs to call their dogs and their men.

And all of a sudden, during this headlong course, my ancestor struck his head against an enormous branch, which literally cleft his skull, and flung him dead on the ground,— while his terrified horse ran away and disappeared in the gathering gloom of the woods.

The younger d'Arville at once drew rein, leaped to the ground, lifted his brother in his arms, and he saw that the brains were running out of the great wound with the blood.

Then he sat down beside the corpse, rested the gory and disfigured head upon his knees, and waited there,—looking at the brother's immobile face. . . . Gradually a fear came upon him,—a singular fear that he had never felt before: the fear of the darkness, the fear of the desolate forest, the fear of solitude, and also the fear of that weird wolf which had killed his brother by way of avenging himself on both of them.

The darkness thickened; the cold made cracklings in the trees. François rose up shuddering, unable to remain there any longer, feeling himself ready to faint. Nothing could be heard,—neither the voices of the dogs, nor the sound of the horns, everything to the invisible horizons seemed dumb; and the solemn silence of the icy evening seemed full of something frightful and strange.

He lifted in his giant arms the great body of Jean, placed it across the saddle, mounted, and rode on slowly, feeling dizzy as if drunk,—haunted by all sorts of hideous and start-ling fancies.

And suddenly a great form passed across the darkening pathway. It was the wolf. A shock of fear tingled through the hunter;—a coldness, as of a trickling of water, descended his back, and, like a monk haunted by a devil, he crossed himself,—startled by this unexpected reappearance of the frightful prowler. But as his eyes fell on the inert corpse lying across the saddle before him, his fear suddenly changed to anger,—he shook with a boundless rage.

Then he spurred his horse, and rushed after the wolf.

He pursued him through thickets and ravines and hedges and woods which he could no longer recognise,—keeping his eye ever fixed upon the white shape flying through the night before him.

His horse also seemed animated by supernatural spirit and vigor. He galloped straight on, with his neck stretched out,—knocking the head and the feet of the dead man, lying across the saddle, against the trees as he passed. Briars tore the hair, the dead forehead spattered the enormous trunks with blood as it battered against them; the spurs tore away the bark.

And suddenly horseman and horse burst from the forest into a valley, just as a crimson moon showed her face above the crags. The valley was stony,—closed in by enormous rocks. There was no issue; and the wolf, brought to bay at last, turned round.

François uttered a yell of joy that the echoes repeated

like a thunder-peal, and leaped from his horse,—cutlass in hand.

The wolf, with spine rounded and bristling, waited for him, crouching;—his eyes scintillated like two stars. But the strong hunter first took his dead brother down from the saddle, seated him upon a rock, and supported his head— now one mass of blood,—with stones,—and thundered into his ears, as if talking to a deaf man:

"Now Jean, you'll have something to look at!—look at this!"

Then he flung himself on the monster. He felt strong enough to overturn a mountain, to crush rock in his hands. The beast strove to bite, to tear his entrails; but he had immediately seized him by the throat, without even a thought of using his weapon; and he began to strangle him slowly, quietly,—listening to the stopping of the breath in the brute's throat, the stopping of the beating of the heart. And he laughed wildly,—enjoying himself monstrously,—gradually tightening his mighty grip more and more,—shouting in the delirium of his joy:—"Look, Jean!—look!" All resistance ceased. The body of the wolf became limp. The wolf was dead

Then François lifted him up bodily, and carried him to the feet of the elder brother, and flung him down before him,— repeating, in a voice of emotion:

"Here—here—here!—my poor Jean!—here he is!"

Then he threw both corpses on the horse, one over the other, and rode home.

He entered the château, laughing and crying, like Gargantua at the birth of Pantagruel,—shouting and stamping for triumph as he related the death of the animal,—sobbing and tearing his beard as he told the death of his brother.

And often afterward, when speaking of that occasion, he would say, with tears in his eyes:

"Ah! but if Jean could only have seen me throttle the other, I'm sure he'd have died glad!"

The widow of my ancestors inspired her orphan son with the horror of hunting,—and it has been transmitted from father to son down to me.

FORGIVENESS

FORGIVENESS

SHE had been brought up in one of those families that live shut up in themselves,—and that always seem out of the way of everything. They know nothing about political events, notwithstanding they talk about them at table;—for them changes in the government are matters which take place at such a distance, that they can only be spoken of as historical facts,—like the death of Louis XVI, or the disembarking of Napoleon.

Customs change, fashions succeed fashions. In such quiet families, where the old traditional manners are always kept up, these changes are never noticed. And if any shocking occurrence happens in the neighbourhood, all the scandal dies away at the threshold of their door. At most, the father and mother may possibly some evening exchange a few words on the subject,—but in a whisper, because even walls have ears. And, discreetly, the father may observe:

"You heard about that shameful affair in the Rivoil family?"

And the mother answers:

"Who could ever have thought it? It is simply frightful."

And the children suspect nothing, and reach the age of life with a bandage over their eyes and reason,—without suspecting what the under side of existence means,—without knowing that people do not think as they speak, do not talk as they act,—without knowing that one must live in a state of continual warfare, or, at best, of armed peace, with everybody,—without ever imagining that one is always sure to be tricked if one is simple, deceived if one is sincere, maltreated if one is kind and good.

Some go on to the moment of their death in this blindness of loyalty, honour and probity,—beings so thoroughly upright that nothing can open their eyes.

Others ultimately disabused, yet unable to understand, are perpetually stumbling here and there in wild desperation; and die at last in the belief that they have been the sport of exceptional ill fortune,—the wretched victims of unlucky circumstances, and of peculiarly evil-hearted men.

The Savignols married their daughter Berthe at the age of eighteen. She married a young man from Paris, named Georges Baron, who was connected with the Exchange. He was a handsome fellow, talked well, had an exterior manner in all respects calculated to inspire confidence; but within himself, he made fun of his old-fashioned parents-in-law, whom he spoke of to his own friends as "My dear fossils."

He belonged to a good family; and his young wife was rich. He took her to Paris to live.

There she became one of that peculiar provincial class so numerous in the metropolis. She remained totally ignorant of the great city,—ignorant of its fashionable society, its pleasures, and its ways,—just as she had always remained ignorant of life, and its perfidies, and its mysteries.

Always shut up in her own household, she knew little of any street except her own; and if she ever ventured into another quarter, it seemed to her like a long voyage to some foreign and unfamiliar city. She would say, in the evening:

"I crossed the boulevards to-day."

Two or three times a year, her husband took her to the theatre. These rare amusements were great events for her, which she never forgot the impression of, and was always talking about.

Sometimes, three months afterward, she would suddenly burst out laughing at table, and cry out:

"Don't you remember that actor in the general's uniform, who crowed like a cock?"

All her acquaintances were limited to two families distantly related to her own, and these two families represented all she knew of humanity. She always spoke of them as "the Martinets" and "the Michelints."

Her husband lived as he pleased, coming home just when it suited him,—sometimes at daylight, always with the pretext of having been very busy; never bothering himself much, however, to find excuses, so certain did he feel that no suspicion could ever enter the candid mind of his wife.

But one morning she received an anonymous letter.

She remained for the moment thunder-struck,—being too upright of heart to comprehend the infamy of denunciation,

to despise the missive whose author pretended to be inspired
by a wish for her happiness, by the hatred of evil, and by
the love of truth.

It was thus revealed to her that her husband had for two
years been intimate with a young widow, Madame Rosset, and
used to pass all his evenings with her.

She did not know how to dissimulate, or to feign, or to spy,
or to lay plans. When he came home to breakfast, she simply
threw down the letter before him, and fled sobbing to her room.
He had ample time to understand, to prepare his answer; and,
having done so, he went and knocked at his wife's door. She
opened it at once,—with her eyes down, not daring to look
at him. He smiled, sat down, took her on his lap; and then in
a gentle, half-mischievous tone, he said:

"My little darling, it is true that Madame Rosset is a friend
of mine: I have known her for ten years and think very
highly of her; and I may also tell you that I know twenty
other families whom I have never talked to you about,—
simply because I know you don't care about society and recep-
tions and introductions, and all that sort of thing. But now,
in order to make an end of all these infamous denunciations,
I beg you will be good enough to dress yourself immediately
after breakfast, and let us make a visit together to this young
lady:—I am sure you will become good friends right off."

She hugged and kissed her husband; and moved by that
feminine curiosity which, once aroused, is not easily put to
sleep again, she did not even refuse to pay a visit to this un-

known woman, of whom she could not help still feeling a little
suspicious. She felt instinctively that a danger, once known, is
half averted.

She entered a pretty little room,—full of charming oddities,
decorated with art,—on the fourth floor of a fine house. After
five-minutes waiting in a drawing-room shadowed by hangings,
draperies, and curtains gracefully arranged, a door opened,
and a young woman appeared,—very dark, small, a little inclined to be stout,—who smiled and looked surprised.

Georges introduced them to each other:

"My wife, Madame Julie Rosset."

The young widow uttered a little cry of astonishment and
joy, and rushed forward holding out both her hands. She had
never hoped, she said, for such good fortune, knowing that
Madame never received visitors; but she was so happy,—so
delighted! She was so fond of Georges (she called Georges
with sisterly familiarity) that she had always been just crazy
to know his little wife, and to be fond of her, too!

Before a month was over the two women had become insep-
arable friends. They saw each other every day, often twice a
day; and dined together every evening, sometimes at one house,
sometimes at the other. Georges now did not absent himself
from home any more,—declared his business no longer occupied all his time, saying that he loved to sit by his own hearth.

Finally, some apartment being vacant in the house occupied by Madame Rosset, Madame Baron at once rented it, so
as to be nearer her friend, and more often with her.

And for two whole years, there followed a cloudless friendship,—a friendship of heart and soul,—absolute, tender, self-sacrificing, delicious. Berthe could scarcely open her mouth without pronouncing the name of Julie, who, to her mind, represented perfection itself.

She lived in happiness,—a perfect, quiet, gentle happiness.

But all of a sudden Madame Rosset became very sick. Berthe never left her side. She sat up with her night after night; her husband himself seemed to share all her anxiety.

Now, one morning, the doctor, after making his usual visit, took Georges and his wife aside, and told them that he considered their friend's condition very serious indeed.

As soon as he was gone, the young couple sat down and looked at each other, in dismay;—then both burst into tears. All that night they watched together beside the bed: and Berthe tenderly kissed the sick woman from time to time:—while Georges, standing at the foot of her bed, watched her all the while without ever moving his eyes from her face.

Next day, she was still worse.

Finally, toward evening, she declared she felt better, and constrained her friends to go down stairs to dinner.

They were sitting in their own apartments, sadly, feeling no inclination to eat anything, when the housekeeper came in and handed Georges a note. He opened it, turned livid; and, rising, said to his wife in a strange manner:—"Wait for me a moment, I must go out: I will be back in ten minutes. Above all things, don't go away!"

And he ran to his room to get his hat.

Berthe waited for him, tortured by a new anxiety. But, obedient in all things, she did not think of reutrning to her friend's room before Georges should return.

As he did not come back, it occurred to her to go to his room, and see if he had taken his gloves, which would be a sign that he had gone out to make a visit.

But the gloves were there; she saw them at the very first glance. Beside them lay a piece of crumpled paper. She recognized that also. It was the note which had just been given to Georges.

And a burning temptation,—the very first she had ever felt in her whole life,—came upon her to read, to find out. Her conscience, revolting, struggled against it; but the gnawing of a painful and terribly excited curiosity urged her on. She took the paper, opened it, and recognized Julie's handwriting, —a trembling scrawl, written in pencil. She read:—"Come by yourself, and kiss me, my poor friend: I am going to die."

At first she did not understand, and stood there stupefied,— being especially shocked by the idea of death. Then, suddenly, the familiar tone of the letter caught her attention; and as in one great lightning-flash, illuminating her whole life, she saw all the infamous truth, all their treason, all their perfidy. She understood their long deceit, their looks, their silent mockery of her good faith, their betrayal of her confidence. She saw them again, each in front of the other at evenings, under the shade of her own lamp, reading the same book, consulting each other with their eyes at the end of each page.

And her heart swollen with indignation, bruised with suffering, sank in a limitless despair.

Footsteps approached;—she fled, and locked herself up in her own room.

A little while after, her husband called her:

"Come quick!—Madame Rosset is dying."

Berthe appeared at her door, and said, with white and trembling lips:

"Go back alone to her!—she has no need of me!"

He stared at her wildly, half-crazed by grief, and repeated:

"Quick! quick!—she is dying."

Berthe replied:

"You would be better pleased if it were me."

Then, perhaps, he understood, and went back alone to the chamber of the dying woman.

He wept for her without dissimulation, without shame,—indifferent to the grief of his wife who no longer spoke to him or looked at him, and lived alone with her disgust for him, in dumb anger,—praying morning and night to God.

Nevertheless, they still lived together, ate together at the same table,—in silence and despair.

Gradually his grief calmed, but she did not forgive him.

And so life went on—terribly unhappy for both of them.

For one year they remained as completely strangers to each

other as if they had never met. Berthe almost went mad.

Then one morning she left the house at dawn, and returned about eight o'clock, carrying in both hands an enormous bouquet of roses,—white roses,—all white.

And she sent word to her husband that she desired to speak to him.

He came, feeling anxious, uneasy.

She said to him:

"We are going out together. Please carry these flowers;—they are too heavy for me."

He took the bouquet, and followed his wife.

A carriage was waiting for them: it started immediately they had taken their seats.

She stopped at the gate of the cemetery. Then Berthe, whose eyes filled with tears, said to Georges:—"Take me to her tomb." He trembled without knowing why, and walked on before her, still carrying the flowers in his arms. Finally he stopped before a white marble, and designated it without saying anything.

Then she took the great bouquet from him, and, kneeling down, laid it at the foot of the grave. Then she prayed for a little while,—prayed suppliantly and silently!

Standing behind her, her husband, haunted by memories, was weeping.

She rose up, and held out her hands to him.

"If you wish," she said, "we will be friends."

THE END